ROCK BAND FIGHTS EVIL #5

THIS WORLD IS NOT MY HOME

ROCK BAND FIGHTS EVIL #5

THIS WORLD IS NOT MY HOME

D.J. Butler

WordFire Press
Colorado Springs, Colorado

ISBN: 978-1-61475-406-0

Cover design by Janet McDonald

Art Director Kevin J. Anderson

Cover artwork images by Carter Reid

Book Design by RuneWright, LLC
www.RuneWright.com

Published by
WordFire Press, an imprint of
WordFire, Inc.
PO Box 1840
Monument CO 80132

Kevin J. Anderson & Rebecca Moesta, Publishers

WordFire Press Trade Paperback Edition June 2016
Printed in the USA
wordfirepress.com

Chapter One

"You're not thinking of trying to get past Herself, are you?" I ask Jim Throat.

The big guy laughs. He's strapping his sword on him like a knight, like you don't see on the Outside anymore except in pictures and parades. "We're late, Twitch, and out of options."

"Late?" I ask. I'm up to my knees in floating wreckage. We all are. It's hilarious, and it doesn't feel like we're *late*. It feels like we're *too late*. The joke's been told. Not only has it been told, but it beat the stuffing out of us all in the telling. My head hurts, I have blood in my hair, and, judging by the scrapes, bruises, and blood on the others, I might have got off easy from our encounter with the boar-headed Prince of Hell, Semyaz, and his thugs in the Silver Eel.

"The equinox," Jim says. "The Liminal Year." I'm not sure what he means. "If you have a better plan, now's the time to tell me."

Adrian Keys already has stuff in his pockets, but he's cramming in more. There's the Eye he has no idea how to use and candles and string and maybe a dead mouse. And that gum he's always chewing. He's got nice breath, Adrian.

"I don't think I can think of a better one," I admit, "but aren't I allowed to feel sad that our choices are so few?"

"Just don't cry," Eddie Guitar grunts. Eddie has one bad eye, and it slides off in the wrong direction as he's talking. He's got stuff in his pockets too, but it isn't wizard-stuff—no dead mice. It's pocketknives and wire and bullets. In his hands he has his long boomer. "You mean Mab, I guess?"

"Close. Only much worse." I have my fighting sticks; that's all I need. We all wade through the ruined restaurant and bar, picking up our stuff after taking a serious beating from some of the major Fallen. There are dead bodies all around, and parts of dead bodies. Some of them look human. The Infernals are funny, all right, though I sort of feel like I'd like to hear a new joke now and then.

"Stop!" says Mike Bass. He's the big one, and the way he's shoving candy bars and booze into his pockets, he plans on getting bigger. "Just for once, can't somebody tell me what's going on ahead of time?"

Jim Throat nods at me. I guess he's done speaking, and no wonder, if we're going to have any stealth in our approach. I don't know if it's true that Jim's father can hear him talking, but Jim seems convinced of it.

"Sure," I say. "There's a special road our Jim here wants to walk, a very old one. We're going to have to go through the Mirror Queendom to get to it, and we'll have to deal with the guardians. The biggest of the guardians is Herself."

"What road?" Eddie asks.

"Guardians?" Mike adds.

"Creatures that will try to stop us. Herself, for instance, is a sort of reptile. The road is the Crossroads. It's the oldest road, and one of the fixed points of the Queendom."

"*Herself* is Rahab the dragon," Adrian Keys says. Adrian always knows just enough to get himself in trouble, and a good deal less than he thinks he knows.

"Dragon?" Mike Bass asks. "Like Sleeping Beauty?"

"Like Isaiah," Eddie Guitar mutters. "Art thou not it that hath cut Rahab, and wounded the dragon?"

"*Cagado*," Mike says. "That sounds bad."

"Nah," Adrian tells him, snapping the chewing gum in his mouth, "it's cause to be optimistic. It's a dragon who can be killed."

"Wounded," says Eddie. "And it doesn't even say wounded *how bad*."

"That's right, big fella," I say to Adrian. "It's cheerful."

Mike looks at me with that hurt look, so I show him udders. It's funny to see him go all red in the face and confused.

"No, it ain't," says Eddie. He stuffs even more boomer shells into the pockets of his jacket, which has the sleeves ripped off it. "Rahab was wounded by the Arm of the Lord. Which we ain't got."

"Thanks," Mike mumbles. "That spark of hope I was feeling disoriented me. I needed someone to kill it."

"'And Miriam the prophetess, the sister of Aaron, took a timbrel in her hand,'" Eddie says. "'And all the women went out after her with timbrels and with dances. And Miriam answered them, Sing ye to the Lord, for he hath triumphed gloriously; the horse and his rider hath he thrown into the sea.'"

"'Song of the Sea,'" Adrian says. "The song of Heaven's triumph over Rahab the chaos dragon."

"What's a timbrel?" Mike asks.

"Go to hell," Eddie tells him.

"Don't feel bad," I say to Mike. I swish my tail to be shiny for the big guy. "If we die, we'll all die together."

Jim holds up the mirror in his hand. I hiss, already feeling the Push against my body, but I don't show it. I'm not really sure I'll be able to get to the Crossroads, but it sounds like a good plan, so I'll try.

I still don't know quite what Jim's hurry is.

"I guess you know the way?" Eddie Guitar asks me.

Ah, Eddie. Always wanting to be sure everything is under control. And the great big fat joke on you, Eddie, is that nothing is ever under control. "Of course."

Adrian says a short incantation and touches the mirror. It opens. I feel the Push immediately, like hands all over my body scratching and punching me and trying to throw me away. The Push makes me feel sad. And lonely.

I try not to let my face show anything. The others won't be able to feel the Push because they're humans, or whatever they are, and not Outcasts. There aren't many Outcasts. You have to really make Mab angry to get thrown out. And if you make her too angry, she just kills you. It's a fine line.

Jim doesn't wait. He grabs the hilt of his sword and steps through. At least he doesn't actually draw it; the Rangers will look on us with enough hostility without our actually having bared weapons in our hands.

"Once more unto the breach," Adrian mumbles. "Et cetera."

Mike Bass is breathing hard. "Keep your eye on the ball, Mike," Eddie tells him, patting him on the shoulder. "We're just passing through, and the destination ain't far."

"That reminds me," I tell them both, and also Adrian. "Don't eat anything." I show them a boy, because I don't want to distract Mike so much that he misses my words. Though that might be very funny.

"Why not?" Mike asks. "Is it poison?"

It is definitely funny to leave him hanging. I fight against the Push and step through the mirror into the Outer Bounds.

In the moment of transition, I spare a tiny thought for Pulse. Is he where I left him? I wonder. He must be. He's probably been laughing his head off without stop since we parted ways.

The light changes immediately. From the weaving, unnatural blue light of the long, skinny bulbs in the bar, it switches to the patchy gloom and dull glow of the Outer Bounds, shafts worming through the darkness from every direction and intersecting in a beautiful yellow-white lattice like a spider's web stretching forever in all directions. It's not home, but it's closer to home than I've been in a long time, and I'm going to get closer still.

I feel … sort of excited.

Two of the Queen's Rangers are already there, leather on their bodies and their legs, tree-and-lightning-bolt symbol on their chests, and weapons in their hands. I know them, and if I didn't, they'd know me.

"Outcast!" hisses the larger one. He's showing a bear, but the tail hanging off his rump might belong to an iguana the size of a horse. Well, getting called names tends to dampen my enthusiasm just a bit. Even if they're technically correct.

"Buzz," I nod to him, and then to his companion. "Flit."

Adrian enters the Outer Bounds behind me, and we both step cautiously aside. We have to make room for Mike and Eddie to join us.

Flit's showing girl to everyone, but she has her fox's tail. Anyway, I'd know her by her face. "You came back once, Twitch Pony," she says. "Mab let you off that time. You shouldn't have come back again."

I shrug, because what else can I do? "Fine."

The Rangers both raise their spears and point them at me. The spears are sharpened wood, so I keep a careful eye on them.

"Fine?" asks Buzz Bear. "We have to kill you."

They both hop from one foot to the other where they stand. They're nervous about Jim. He glares at them, then leans back to rap hard against the mirror out of which we've just stepped.

"You, though," Flit says, pointing her spear at Jim. "You come with us."

Eddie Guitar slides through the gate. He pumps his boomer as he steps into the Outer Bounds and puts on an I-mean-business face. He looks around at the staircases arching overhead and the shafts falling through the floor and the passages that seem to bend away and come back to the same point before Outside geometry would permit them.

"No one's actually shooting at us," he says. "That's nice for a change."

"*Yet*," says Adrian. "Give them a minute."

Mike touches the ground immediately at his shoulder. Mike has his shooter out, too. "I've seen you eat … human food," Mike says to me. "Why can't I eat … uh, fairy food?"

The gate closes behind Mike.

"I had to get used to it," I tell him. "The first thing I ate was a Chocodile, and I thought I was going to die."

"No!" squeals Flit Fox. "You don't have a minute, and you can't eat! Abandon the Outcast and the half-devil and get out of the Mirror Queendom."

They know who Jim is. They're scared of him, but they want him.

And they're hesitating. I guess it's because they worry about the Outsiders I have with me. As they should. My Outsider friends aren't just any ordinary companions; they're a rock-and-roll band.

I show the falcon, and I spring high into the air. I find a stone lintel that juts out far enough, and I perch on its edge. The Outer Bounds around me wheeze and scuttle, making the slow groaning sound that comes from so much stone shifting on its thousand, thousand axes.

Flit shows a swallow, and with two flaps of her wings, she joins me on the lintel. It's wide, too wide to be comfortable because Flit shows girl again and points her spear at me. It's lethal, that wood is, not blunted by Outsider hands and smelting. I ease out my fighting sticks and show Flit my teeth. She shows hers back. It might be romantic, except that we're armed and we both mean business.

"We're too many," I say to Flit. "Don't even try it. Do you want to be hurt?" I mean it. I don't want to injure Flit Fox or any of Mab's Rangers. I'm in enough trouble as it is. I just want to get through as quickly as I can.

Flit fidgets. She waits, keeping her spear between us.

Below us, Buzz roars. He lunges forward on all fours, teeth snapping.

Jim is ready for him. The tall singer steps to one side, and he avoids the easy mistake. He leaves his sword at his belt and just kicks Buzz in the muzzle. When Buzz yelps and falls forward onto his face, Jim Throat grabs him and drags him across the chamber. It doesn't pay to underestimate Jim.

Flit stabs at me, and I catch the spear. "Wrong move," I tell Flit, and then I show her the pony. I kick with my rear legs, knocking her wings-over-tail off the lintel. The spear falls clattering to the floor and I fall with it. I slow my fall by showing the falcon and glide to a landing showing girl. Easy. I'm very good at this.

"*Caray*," says Mike. He's right. This is not a promising start.

Jim throws Buzz Bear down a hole in the floor and waits. When Buzz reappears two seconds later at the edge of the well, showing lizard and frantically scrabbling for a grip, Jim pounds the Ranger in the snout with a clenched fist. He knocks Buzz spinning back down into the well.

"And stay down!" Eddie snorts. He's still standing with his boomer, looking tough.

"You won't escape the Rangers, devil's son!" Flit Fox yells, and zips out of sight under a low arch. Her warning is unnecessary. Buzz's roar has already alerted all the Rangers in earshot, and that's likely to be very many of them. Flit will be back, and she won't be alone.

"Which way?" Adrian asks me. He could probably figure it out if he had to, he's clever enough with languages and magic spells and secret stuff, but as it happens, I know where to go.

"In," I tell them, and I cut past two false hallways and into a doorway that they don't see. It's showing wall, but I know it's a door, and I step right into it.

"Damn," Eddie mutters, but he's smart enough to follow me.

Mike Bass's teeth chatter as he steps in through the door. "This Rahab," he asks. "Is it in the Moses half of the Bible?"

"Why do you care?" I ask. Silly book. All books are silly, vain attempts to put pins through reality to make it hold still, when it won't, might as well pin water to a board. But any book written by someone who's that desperate for you to see him as the hero, well, you know it won't be trustworthy.

Mike puts his hand in the pocket of his leather jacket. He's holding on to one of the bottles he picked out of the wreckage of the restaurant, I guess. "Dunno," he says. "Everything from the Moses half just seems meaner."

"If you're hoping someone's going to tell you that Rahab's a big softy," Eddie says, chewing his words because he thinks they're so good, "it ain't gonna happen." Even here, his bad eye slides to the side every few minutes. He sees visions, Eddie does, and they aren't happy ones.

"I'm just hoping that one thing, for once, will turn out to be easy."

Adrian laughs. "You're in the wrong band."

I lead them past three archways, each taller than the last. They look tempting, with light spilling down from windows high above into broad courtyards, and I can smell cinnamon, but I know they're traps. I know this place. Besides, I can hear the breathing, and the echoing thumps of feet and paws.

Instead I turn sideways to edge through a crack in the wall. Three arm-lengths in, it opens up, and I find myself standing on a wide mezzanine. A stone balustrade keeps me from a long drop, and stairs roll down, double-wide, to the floor below. Beyond the stairs are a chasm in the floor and a bridge across it.

Massed on the stairs are a dozen Rangers. They crouch fiercely, protected by layers of leather and a bristling wall of wooden spikes.

Flit Fox is one of them. She stands slightly behind the others, raising her spear and pointing it at me.

"Twitch Pony!" she cries. "Outcast! Surrender now!"

Here we go. I ignore her because of the silly things she says. Instead, I show them the falcon and leap into the air.

A rattling storm of wings shakes the Outer Bounds, and many of the Rangers follow. Rooks, starlings, thrushes, mockingbirds, and even an owl fight among themselves for airspace, snapping after me. The room behind me sounds like an enormous cloak having the dust shaken out of it by its giant owner.

I swoop close to the wall, where ornamental columns are staggered in climbing rows. Their pedestals and capitals are leering skulls, stone flames in their eyes and tongues lolling over their crumbling teeth. I'd laugh if I weren't so occupied. Instead, I show girl, kick my heels into the forehead of one of those skulls, and take my fighting clubs into my hands as I spring back at my foes.

This surprises them. I laugh and lay about me, *thump-a-ta-thump-thump!*, a basic, bouncy little rhythm, and Hop Badger tumbles out of his badger-tailed crow showing, hitting the ground with a heavy thud as I land beside him on my toes. I roll forward with the fall, ignoring Hop's groans, and swing around me again. Another of the Queen's Rangers falls, clutching her head, and then I show the falcon once more. I flap my wings and push through a descending hail of feathers to head in the opposite direction, ceilingward, past and beyond them.

Mab's Rangers mostly train to fight Outsiders who get lost and lucky, or terribly unlucky, depending on your point of view, and accidentally come into the Outer Bounds. Outcasts are rare, and Outcasts who try to return are rarer still. The Rangers are well armed, but they're not really ready for me.

They're not really ready for Jim Throat, either. As I swoop above the staircase, owl pecking at my long tail, I see that Jim's taken Flit Fox's spear away from her. He's beating the Rangers around him with it, the wood bruising them where steel would be unable. He could easily be stabbing them with the poky end, so the fact that he isn't means he's deliberately holding back. He doesn't want to anger Mab and Oberon, maybe. The Rangers reassemble showing birds and swarm back at him, but then Eddie Guitar is at Jim's side, raising his weapon.

BOOM!

It's a loud gun anywhere. Inside this stone chamber, it's enough to wreck one's hearing. The slug tears through the cloud of flying Rangers. If they were normal birds, they'd be on the stone and dying, but because they're really Mab's children, instead they're knocked back in the air, leaving Jim free to keep wreaking havoc with his borrowed stick.

Adrian and Mike come up at the rear. The big guy keeps poking Adrian in the ribs, which probably means he's trying to stop the wizard from falling asleep. Adrian doesn't sleep more than other men. He just sleeps at all the wrong times, poor boy. He's looking through the Eye, muttering as he does, and clutching his bit of candle wax. I'll have to stay out of his way if I don't want to get my tail singed. When he comes through, Adrian comes through in a big way.

Jim crashes down through the Rangers. He looks all wrong, wearing his jeans and his loose, long-sleeved shirt almost like a tunic or a blouse. He looks out of place, but he rolls through the Rangers like the Juggernaut. He hits the bottom of the stairs as I circle around the mezzanine again, landing and showing the pony.

Buzz Bear is at the top of the stairs. He's decided to leave the Outsiders alone and face me. He's bruised about the face and his tail is kinked, which is probably why he looks so unhappy.

"You don't belong here anymore, Pony," Buzz growls. "Can't you see that?"

He stabs at me and I rear up, lashing out with my front hooves. I knock him back a pace or two and then for good measure I kick out backward, too. I don't know what I hit, but it yelps.

I quickly switch to showing girl and flash my teeth at him, waving my fighting sticks in invitation. "Why not, Buzz?" I ask him. I spin around and poke Amble Owl in the throat with one of my sticks. He goes down with gargle. Others are with him, and I pound one or two and then spin aside, getting under Buzz's next attack. I throw him into his friends and retreat to the top of the stairs.

"Look at what you're doing!" Buzz's face is purple, he's mad. "You're invading the Queendom!"

"No, I'm not," I say, and I mean it. I borrow Eddie's words. "I'm just passing through. Stay out of my way, and no one will get hurt."

But they aren't getting in my way, not most of them. Most of them are trying to pile on to Jim Throat. I see from the top of the stairs that I've only distracted a few of them, and the rest are after him.

Maybe it's because he's in front, I tell myself, and I take a few quick swipes at Buzz. He shows bear and snaps at me with really big teeth, but I'm too quick for that. I show falcon in a split second, and a flap of my wings takes me over his head. I show boy against the wall and kick off against it, pounding Buzz in the face with my fighting sticks. Girl is more acrobatic, but boy has stronger arms. Buzz is not going to feel good tomorrow.

But maybe it isn't that, after all. Maybe all they really want is Jim.

I shove a stick down Buzz's craw, forcing him back, and I point down at Jim with the other. "You'll never get it, you know," I say to him. "It's his by right, really. Best give up now and get out of our way."

The light in his eyes tells me Buzz knows what I'm talking about. It also tells me he isn't happy, so I show girl and jump back to the balustrade. He lunges, still showing bear. That's a fierce form, all right, with lots of teeth, but I leap high into the air and he misses.

I flip backward. It feels good, so I flip right back over the balustrade and show falcon so I can glide to the ground. Buzz Bear and Amble Owl poke spears at me, but they miss. While they've been drilling in the Queendom's gardens and throwing out wandering apprentice wizards like so many bouncers, I've been dodging Zvuvim and the Fallen. They're no match for me.

They might be a match for Jim, though. Only because there's an awful lot of them.

He charges into a knot of Rangers on the narrow stone bridge. More Rangers rush him from behind, and I see Mike and Eddie ducking out of the way as Adrian raises a handful of his pocket trash.

I show falcon and veer to the side.

"*Per Volcanum ignem mitto!*" Adrian shouts. That one's his favorite. It's big and showy, and it packs a real kick.

A gout of flame explodes out of his candle and the Eye. It knocks down several of the Rangers, and they don't get up.

Most of the others run, scattering with singed tails in all directions. My own tail feels warm, and as I land on the far side of the chasm, I check it; its tips are black and crisp.

"Mab's pointy teeth!" I snap.

Adrian has done well, and so now he crumples over. Mike has him by his shiny silver jacket and is trying to keep the wizard from falling into the chasm. That's good, this is a deep one, and Adrian Keys doesn't have a flying form to show. He's more of a stand-in-place-and-draw-circles sort of wizard, who can once in a while let fly a good bang.

I show falcon and cross to the bridge to help. I land showing pony and whinny to get Mike's attention. Mike slings Adrian across my back and steadies him.

Behind me, the Rangers regroup. I hear Eddie pay them some close attention.

BOOM! BOOM! BOOM!

The boomer won't kill them, not unless Eddie's loaded in some strange ammunition, but it'll sting, so they'll duck and try to stay out of the way, and if they get hit they'll be knocked back. I move forward. Adrian's snoring body on my back makes me more aware of the Push that continues to operate against me, shoving at me with every step. It'll get worse once we're out of the Outer Bounds, and again I wonder about my ability to actually get to the Crossroads like Jim plans.

I snort to show I don't care, and I follow Jim.

He slams one Ranger's head against the floor and then flings her into the air. The Ranger shows dazed whooping crane and sags in a descending circle over the crevasse before she manages to crumple onto the stone floor behind me. Jim kicks another Ranger who isn't so lucky and shows basset hound as he goes yipping down into the darkness.

For just a moment, the way ahead is clear.

But then I hear a terrible buzzing sound.

Chapter Two

"Nuts!" Eddie barks.

"Again?" Mike Bass asks. "I thought we lost that guy in New Mexico!"

"Might not be the same one." Eddie pumps his boomer.

"How does that make me feel better?"

"Making you feel better isn't my job," Eddie growls. "I just book the gigs and play the chords."

Jim Throat strides out onto the far side of the bridge. Before him is a row of arches, each coming down in a tip like a stalactite, melting and flowing into a stalagmite base rising from the floor. Behind the arches are open passageways, and whipping up one of those is a cloud of flies.

Really big flies. Flies the size of large dogs. With clacking metal mandibles.

"Mab's belly button." We've seen these things before.

Jim draws his sword, and about time.

I realize I'm last, and I look over my pony shoulder. Hop Badger and Amble Owl and the others are regrouping. There's no time to waste.

"This way!" I call to the band. They hear it just as a whinny, but they must see me flashing past and racing into a narrow, shadowed corner of the portico. It doesn't look like a passage because it isn't lit, but I know it's one anyway. I race into the darkness, careful not to let Adrian fall off my back.

I hear pounding feet behind me, which must be the band—they all run too heavy to be any of Mab's folk, and the flap of wings is distant and behind them. Then I hear *BOOM, BOOM, BOOM* and *BANG, BANG*, and the noise is thunder, so loud that the walls of the passage shudder, trying to cover their ears.

Ahead there's an exit. I'm no expert in things Infernal—if I were, I'd have known about their inability to take a joke, and I might have avoided my Gigantic Colossal Mistake and still been welcome in the Queendom. But I remember that Zvuvim are creatures of darkness. They can't take daylight, it melts them right into nothing. Their master-spawner, the Baal, doesn't like it either.

Adrian could get us some light, he's done it before, but he's asleep.

Still, I know the way out. And in the Queendom, it's always day.

Ahead of me is a spiral staircase. I need to get on it and head down, but four Queen's Rangers suddenly come racing up from one side and array themselves in front of me. Two of them show bobcat and raccoon, which don't worry me much. But the others show ape and rhinoceros, and unless I get very lucky, I'm not going to be able to just run past them.

But I decide I'd better try.

I don't want the ape to wrap its arms around me, nor do I want the rhino's horn in my flank. I aim between them, hoping that neither one of them will be able to stop me. Behind me is all *BOOM, BOOM* still, and I lower my head, scraping against the rhinoceros and feeling my side abrade like I'm being rubbed with a file. The ape grabs, but I'm too fast and he misses, and I'm through.

I'm on the other side, laughing and showing boy at the top of the stairs, with a fighting stick in each hand, before I realize that the ape wasn't grabbing at me after all.

He flashes me funny teeth and slings Adrian over his shoulder.

"Ooh-ooh-ooh," he says. It's a joke. He's stolen my wizard, and now he's making monkey sounds to tease me. I have to admit, it's kind of funny, but I don't laugh. Behind him, Mike Bass and Eddie Guitar are getting closer. Jim is behind them, poking flies out of the air with his sword.

I shrug. "Keep him," I say, and I turn to go down the stairs—

Then I spin suddenly. I fling one of the fighting sticks under my arm. It flies straight, like a skipped stone off a flat lake.

Wham! I smack the ape in his eyeball. He hisses, drops Adrian, and then shows skinny green snake as he slithers away.

Adrian hits the floor hard, poor fella. "Mmmmph?" he asks.

I show pony to kick the rhinoceros in the side of his head because he's looking at his buddy, the ape. Then I grab my thrown fighting stick off the floor and I slap the two of them together, on opposite sides of Slip Bobcat's neck, just as she jumps up and tries to kick me. Her kick fizzles out, and she sinks to the floor, choking.

But then Dodge Raccoon lunges at me, and his spear is out. He's clever, he's let the others take the damage and exhaust me, and he's jumping in for the kill. I'm not going to be able to get out of the way, and my sticks are in the wrong position to block.

This is going to hurt.

BOOM!

Dodge flies sideways. The boomer shell is too worked, too man-made to really hurt him, but the impetus of the little hunk of metal is enough to throw the Ranger down the stairs, squeaking.

For good measure I pummel Slouch Rhinoceros in the face several times. He's so stunned he shows girl and then passes out.

"You're almost late!" I say to Eddie. It isn't a very good joke, but it's all I can come up with at the moment. I'm distracted because the Zvuvim are not only following Eddie, they're also swarming at me from somewhere else.

"There's a second Baal here," Eddie grumbled. He blows three of the big flies into black papery shreds with a single pull of the trigger of his boomer. They're thick around us now, and I pound them before I crouch to grab Adrian Keys.

"Down the stairs!" Mike shouts, and fires his shooter. He's right. I can hear the second Baal Zavuv coming, heavy footsteps. The stone shrinks away from his touch, it isn't right for the Infernals to be here. Not that it's the first time, of course.

Grrrwwaaaaaragh!

The squealing noise makes my tail stand up. It means Jim has managed to poke the first Baal and the beastie isn't happy about it.

"Come on, love," I say to Adrian. I show him lovely girl, warm-peace-sunshine-happiness-and-I-love-you-you-silly-wizard, and I stroke his face. He's not bad-looking, for an Outsider who always shows the same thing. "Wake up now and give us a nice spell."

"Gah." Adrian struggles, but he's forcing his eyes open now.

"What is it, Twitch?" he asks.

"A little light, darling." I show him tender, smiling girl, and he smiles back.

He digs into his pocket and pulls out the Eye. "Easy-peasy," he says, "and so on."

BOOM! Eddie Guitar and his boomer shatter a Zavuv chittering behind my shoulder. Jim's close.

"Now would be good," I suggest warmly.

Adrian grins like it's nothing. And it should be nothing, only every time he tries to do anything that matters, Adrian Keys risks falling asleep. "*Per Isidem Lux*," he says, waving the Eye.

And that's it, daylight. The dark columns and shadowed niches are all suddenly bathed in yellow light like it's noon in the Outer Bounds, where it's never usually anything but twilight. The demon-flies buzz, they're in pain. They swarm this way and that, scattering to get out of the light. Some of them make it. Others don't, and they melt away into nothing.

Slip Bobcat yowls. It might be surprise or it might be a war cry. Either way, big Mike kicks the Ranger and sends her flying down the stairs. She lands on the face of the second Baal Zavuv, just as he's trying to shield his eyes. Suddenly his fly-eyed, pig-tusked head, gray-black and mummified-looking, is wearing a bobcat fur cap. That bites and scratches.

He stumbles back into the darkness, teeming with his fly horde progeny.

"Which way?" hollers Eddie. He's dragging Adrian to his feet. I keep showing girl to Adrian and smiling at him, trying to distract him from the angry buzz of flies and the bellow of a rhinoceros trying to climb to its feet.

"Downstairs," I tell him, and I shrug an apology.

"There's a monster down there!" Mike shouts. *BANG, BANG!* He fires his shooter down the stairs, into the darkness that's alive with flies and their lord.

"Upstairs, then!" I laugh. "It all goes to the same place!" That's not really true, but it's funny to see the looks on their faces, and I have an idea.

The wizard's eyes start to flutter. Eddie slaps him, which only sends him to sleep.

The light snuffs out.

"*Fundillo!*" Mike grabs Adrian and slings him over his shoulder. That's fine, it frees me up.

I show falcon and race up the stairs. I strafe the raccoon and the rhinoceros as I go, raking them with warning claws to remind them that I'm dangerous and that I'll be back, and then I'm wheeling past Mike, who huffs and puffs, and around the staircase. The boomer starts going off again below me.

The stairs up are lit by windows beneath each step, which makes everyone's face look strange and cavernous, gaping eye sockets and mouths. "Don't imagine this light will help you," I call out as a reminder, but of course I'm showing falcon and all the band will hear is a bird's cry.

At the top of the stairs is a long hall. I touch down and show girl, fighting sticks in both hands. Six Rangers charge in my direction across the hall, a leopard and a wolfhound and others I don't immediately make out because they're coming too fast.

"Wake up Adrian!" I yell to Mike as he shuffles to the top, and I run at the Rangers.

They're too many, I don't like the odds. Naturally, I run right for the biggest, fiercest looking one of the lot, and that's the leopard. "Fool!" she snarls.

Two of her fellows are showing boy. I know them, they're Skip Robin and Shudder Mole. They're holding nets and running at the outside of the pack. I can't afford to get into a fight, or I'll get myself tangled up in rope.

I have to keep moving.

The leopard leaps and I leap too. I throw myself at the floor under her feet, and at the same moment I show falcon. The cool stone floor whizzes beneath me just under my feathered breast, and I fly underneath the leopard. Claws slam into the floor on either side of me from above.

I bank sharply to the right once I've passed beneath her, swerving towards the stone wall and then swerving right again.

The wolfhound leaps for me, misses, and then Shudder Mole throws her net. Dog and net together collide into the wall and fall to the floor.

I show girl, which has me running on the wall for two steps before I tumble to the floor and land in a crouch. Jim fights at the top of the stairs with his sword. Dead flies lie around his feet like nutshells or the rinds of eaten fruit, and he stabs at the Baal Zavuv, keeping it from coming out. Fortunately, the stairs are narrow enough and the Baal Zavuv is big enough that only one of them can come up at a time. I think. It's also fortunate that Jim is so good. Good as he is, though, he won't last much longer, even with Eddie at his side pumping boomer shells down the stairs.

I can barely hear myself, even though I yell. "Wake Adrian up!" I point at the wall. My head hurts from all the noise. "Tell him he has to open a hole right *there!*"

I hope that'll work.

And then a net falls over me.

But only over my back and haunches. It doesn't quite cover me, and when I switch instantly to showing pony, it covers me even less. Mike shakes Adrian. I kick back, and I feel my hooves kick into flesh and bone.

I bolt forward. A spear jabs me in the haunch, and it hurts, but then I'm away from the attacker. The net snags on my rump, and I drag it with me.

"Ummph!" yells one of the Rangers behind me. I hear the thud of someone hitting the floor, and I feel weight. I look back. The leopard charges me, and two other Rangers have their hands tangled in the net. They're climbing it like a ladder on the ground, dragging themselves in my direction.

I run. I gallop into a mass of flies, champing with my teeth and throwing my head around like a club. I knock some of them out of the way and keep their mandibles from my face, which is good.

But they land on my back and bite.

It hurts. I can feel myself bleed. Their jaws look like harmless steel, but cut into me like lethal bone.

Into me, and into the rope strands of the net.

I feel the weight suddenly lift as the Zvuvim cut through the ropes and the net disintegrates. Immediately I show a girl and somersault forward. Confused flies bounce away from me, and I slam into them with my fighting sticks, crushing eyes and wings and legs with every swipe.

Eddie backs away from the stairs, reloading shells into his boomer. Jim backs with him, and I see both Baalim squeezing out of the top of the stairs. They're big and gray and man-shaped, like ogres, but they have eyes like enormous flies and tusks like wild pigs. And they reek. Where Jim has cut them or Eddie has plugged them with his boomer, they leak black ooze. In the ambiguous, criss-crossing shafts of light that leave the hall a dull gray, I can see tiny flies bubble in the ooze.

"Now!" I yell.

Spring Leopard charges me with a spear tucked under her arm, its sharp end pointed right at my chest. Behind her come two more Rangers, one on each wing. I brace myself and bring my sticks into position.

Mike punches Adrian in the face. He yells something in Spanish, and it doesn't sound very happy.

I charge. I yell as I go, "Here's Johnny!" I saw that on television once on the lips of a crazy man, and it was hilarious. Also, Spring Leopard won't know what it means, so it might confuse her.

I think I hear Adrian's voice, but I can't make out what he's saying.

I jump and show falcon.

But one of the Rangers jumps before I do. It's the wolfhound, he got out of the net somehow, and his jaws clamp down on my shoulder. I gasp and show pony. In the same moment, he shows boy, and his arms are wrapped around my strong white neck. We fall to the ground hard. I was not prepared for this and I land badly, on my side and tumbling.

Spring Leopard stabs me. Then I roll over the spear and shatter it with the weight of my body. I feel the splinters in my flesh, and then she shows me her leopard. At the same moment the other one shows wolfhound, and they pile on top of me, tearing and biting.

This really isn't funny.

BANG! BANG!

Something bowls the wolfhound away from me. Slugs from Mike's shooter, I guess. I show girl just as Snow Leopard does, and we roll to a stop. I'm on top of her with my hand at her throat, and I punch her right in her button nose.

She lies still. I really hurt.

"Thanks, Mikey," I say to him. He ignores my words and shoots past me, I guess at the other Rangers. The little brass shells from his weapon rain down around me, stinging when they hit my face. I drag myself to my feet. I'll have to pluck splinters from my hip and butt later, but right now I don't have the time.

"Mike," he says. He jams more rounds into his shooter.

"Per Janum portam aperio!"

I see Adrian. He stands, Eye in one hand and looking through it, chanting and waving his fingers at the wall, right where I pointed. As the last of his words leave his lips, the wall parts like eyelids opening. Light streams in, not the gray light coming through every mirrorgate in the Outer Bounds, but the golden-green-blue-red light of day in the Queendom.

Relief. It worked.

Adrian's legs buckle.

"Adrian, baby!" I call to him with my silveriest voice. I show him a girl picnicking beside a stream and shove my arm under his to try to catch him. My rump hurts, and so does my head. I need a long rest in a cool, quiet place, and I don't think I'm going to get one today.

"Twitch?" he says in that woozy voice that means he's not quite asleep yet.

Mike's shooter explodes again in my ear. Zvuvim buzzing around me splatter into wisps of dried carapace and husk, falling apart as the beams of light touch them. The Baalim shriek, outraged. They stagger back. Jim presses the attack, stabbing them with the sword he has in one hand and swinging some wiggling, flailing, unhappy object in the other.

The object complains loudly and changes shape. I see that it is Flit and that Jim has her firmly by the tail as he pounds her into the face of the nearest Baal Zavuv again. Flit yowls. She's having a bad day. Ah, well. I told her I didn't want her to get hurt, and she should stand aside.

"Come on, handsome," I whisper into Adrian's ear.

"I'm awake," he insists, and stumbles towards the light.

I help him get through the opening. It's a circle, just opened up in the wall, so we have to pick up our feet a bit to step through it. On the outside is a rooftop, sloping gently down just beneath the hole. Its tiles are baked clay, and they hold firm as we step onto them. The daylight warms my skin out here, and a gentle breeze tickles me under the ears. The sweet smell of rotting matter fills my nostrils. My bottom still hurts.

"Mikey!" I call. "Mike!" I add, since it's funny to call him *Mikey* but maybe now is not the time to provoke him into doing something stupid.

Mike Bass galumphs our way. He stops at the opening and turns to fire some more. Even standing outside the Outer Bounds, the noise of all the gunfire happening within is still deafening. I look over the edge of the rooftop and see the tops of trees. That's good. Depending on the trees, of course, we might still be a mile off the ground, but it could always be worse. If you force them to, the Outer Bounds go up forever.

Eddie backs up to the opening too. They both smell like the bitter smoke that pours from their weapons.

"Jim!" Eddie yells. I doubt Jim can even hear him over the riot. "Get over here, dammit!"

Mike shuffles out through the opening like an ape. He teeters on the roof and almost loses his balance, which is less like an ape and more like a clown, but then he recovers and sets about putting more ammunition into his shooter.

Eddie is smoother. He takes jerky, deliberate steps, and when Amble Owl gets around a boomer blast and comes at him, Eddie swings the butt-end up the boomer up and clocks Amble right in one of his owl eyes. He shows boy and falls to the floor, crying. Eddie knees Amble in the face and kicks him back into darkness.

I move with Adrian closer to the edge.

"You ready to close the door, sweetie?" I whisper to him, showing him proud lover. I show him this one a lot. It makes him feel powerful, which is what the band usually needs from Adrian Keys.

He nods, adjusts his grip on the Eye.

Mike and Eddie unload a fusillade of thunder into the hole and then pull back. Jim vaults through, lands on the rooftop, and spins to face the threats behind him. He still has his sword in one hand and Flit in the other.

"Now!" I shout, but Adrian is already waving his fingers.

"*Per Janum portam claudio!*"

A pair of gray arms lunge from the opening and grab Jim Throat. Jim smashes at the bug eyes above them with the hilt of his sword. The Baal shrieks, I don't know whether from the pain of being clobbered or the pain of being burned by the light.

Jim struggles, pounding the basket hilt of his sword against the Baal's knuckles repeatedly. He skins the monster, and black ooze spatters Jim's shirt.

The Baal squeezes tighter. Jim stabs the Baal in the shoulder, twisting the point of his sword in the wound.

Grrrrraaaaaaraaaaaarrgh!

The Baal shrieks, but he doesn't let go. He yanks Jim inside as the opening shrinks. He slams Jim's head against the wall and Jim goes slack, dropping his sword and the trembling body of Flit Fox on the tile before he's dragged into darkness.

Eddie grabs at Jim's boots and misses.

Adrian collapses to the tiles, unconscious.

Then the hole closes and Jim is gone.

Chapter Three

"No!"

Eddie raises his boomer to his shoulder and fires into the blank stone wall repeatedly. Sparks fly and he gouges out chips of rock, but the opening doesn't reappear. In the sudden silence the shots are enormous, and birds scatter from the branches nearest the rooftop.

Then I see that Adrian is sliding. "Mike!" I yell, and grab Adrian. I could show pony, which would make me really big and heavy so I could just bite Adrian's pant leg and keep him on the rooftop, but if the tiles give way, we'll both fall. I can show falcon before I hit the ground, but Adrian can't. Especially not when he's asleep.

The Eye *chinks* onto the tile. I grab it with one hand, and with the other I scramble for purchase. I can't hold him, though, he's going over—

And then big Mike Bass is there, grabbing Adrian by one ankle and hauling him to safety with a loud grunt.

"*Mierda,*" Mike curses.

He sounds far away and muffled, like I'm hearing him from the other side of a practicing drum corps. It's sort of funny, so I laugh.

"Adrian!" Eddie yells, and rushes over to shake the wizard. "Adrian, the wall!"

I step out of the way so the boomer's not pointed at me. Eddie's distraught, and I've got enough bruises.

Adrian snores. I can barely hear it over the ringing in my ears from all the gunfire in the Outer Bounds.

I'm not in the Outer Bounds anymore, though. This is the Mirror Queendom proper. This is home, sort of. I look around.

There's no sun because the whole sky is the sun, and it's streaked with every conceivable color that shines. Even black. The black is the shiniest part, not dark at all. The ground's not so far down as it might have been, but I can only see it as shadow among the plants. The trees are tallish but no taller than Outsider trees get. Maybe a hundred feet, and I see places where even mediocre climbers can simply grab a branch and lift themselves into the trees. The climber would have to mind the serpents, of which there are approximately a million, hanging from every branch, but I think the lads' guns will work just fine on the wriggly creatures. We can climb down, no problem.

We'll have to watch out for Wild Things.

Below is a great thicket. I can't see the extent of it, but that doesn't matter here as much as it does Outside. There will be a path, assuming I can overcome the Push. The thorns are long, though. As long as my arm, I think, growing out of branches as thick as my leg. Maybe this improvised exit was better than using one of the regular doors, after all. Except that we lost Jim.

Jim. And the hoof. I turn around.

"Wake up!" Eddie is shouting much too loud. His hearing is probably battered by the gunfire too. He carries earplugs in the stuff in his pockets, I know, because he puts them in when he plays guitar. Maybe he has them in now and that's why he's shouting.

"Eddie," I say, "that's loud."

"Is it?" He yells at me now, and the veins stand out in his neck and at his temples. "Is it too loud for you, Twitch? Maybe it's so loud even Jim can hear! Maybe it's so loud that if you flew around this, this," he flails with one arm at the Outer Bounds, "this building, you could still hear me while you were looking for another way in."

I look up at the Outer Bounds. From this side, it looks like an infinitely tall castle wall. It has roofs and balconies, catwalks, parapets, battlements, gargoyles, rain gutters, and stairs, but it has no apparent upper end. And no windows or doors.

"No," I say, "the ways in are all below us."

Eddie glares at me. "Adrian!" He shakes the little wizard so hard I worry he might accidentally throw him off the rooftop. Accidentally or on purpose. Eddie is very unhappy right now.

Adrian takes no notice. He keeps snoring.

"He's out," I say, "and Jim's gone. We're not going to catch up with him, not that way."

"The Beel … zeboov," Mike says slowly. He's still the new guy. He always will be, until we get a new member; that's how the band is. "What's he doing here?"

Eddie stops shaking Adrian and looks at me.

"It's a good question," I admit. "Do you think they could have followed us all the way from New Mexico?"

"No," Eddie says immediately. "No, I don't."

"I don't either," I agree. "Which means they were waiting here for us."

"Do Azazel and Mab have an alliance?" Eddie looks at me with hard eyes.

"No," I tell him, but I look down at my feet. "No, but there are sometimes dealings, as, you know, there might be between any great powers."

"What are you hiding?" Mike asks.

"Hiding?" It's a bit embarrassing to be caught out by Mike Bass. He's the slow one. No, I remind myself, he's not really slow. He's just new. It isn't the same thing at all. "Ah, look, it's nothing. It's just … well, the reason I'm an Outcast, you see, it has to do with the Infernals. I was a sort of official escort to one of the Princes once, when he visited, and he didn't appreciate my sense of humor."

"Escort?" Mike gulps. "You mean … ?"

"No," I say, "that's not what I mean at all. I mean I was one of the horses pulling Belial's chariot. And I … I arranged for a special set of trumpets to blow him a welcome, see? And, look, never mind, it means nothing. Only that sometimes Mab treats with Hell, and maybe she's doing it in our case."

"Trumpets?" Mike asks.

"Holy shit," Eddie mutters. He shakes his head. "You were pulling the chariot of one of the Princes of Hell, and you farted at him."

Memories. I try not to smile too big. "A lot of us did, actually. It was pretty funny." So funny that someone had to take the blame.

"But why?" Mike puts his hand in his pocket. He's got it wrapped around a flask or a candy bar, I bet.

I shrug. "I like funny things."

"No, I mean … why would Belial … ? I don't get it."

"It doesn't matter," Eddie says. "What matters is Jim."

"Right," I agree. "So isn't it useful that Jim has left us someone to help?"

Flit Fox is groggy. She's so groggy that although she's showing girl, she flickers into fox and back again every couple of seconds. And no wonder, her face looks like it's been used as a club on a monster with a physique like a brick wall. Which it has.

I grab her by her hair.

"Anybody have any cold iron?" I ask.

"What?" Mike is confused.

"True iron. The meteoric stuff. Star metal. Unforged, you know?"

Mike's expression is still blank.

"Newbie," I mutter.

"Check the wizard's pockets," Eddie says. He delivers the line like an order, but he does the searching himself. When he finds a thin, sharp bit of iron, like a razor, and shows it to us, I grin and try not to back away.

I remember the Marked Woman leaning over me, pushing just such a blade against my throat as the tattoos on her face swirled about like threats and curses. That wasn't funny, not the tiniest bit.

"Very good." I show teeth. "Now, follow my lead."

I kick Flit Fox in the belly, and when she sits up, eyes bulging out, I grab her before she can do anything.

"Show your sparrow," I say, "and my demonic familiar here will kill you."

Flit's eyes gape. For a moment I think I've got her.

Then: "That's no demonic familiar. It's just a human, of the kind with lots of pigment! What kind of idiot do you think I am?"

Well, it was worth a try. I carefully conceal my disappointment.

Eddie's boot slams onto the tile next to Flit's head, and suddenly he presses the cold iron up against her face. It's quick enough, and his snarl is ugly enough, that I'm taken by surprise. I feel nervous. "Show your sparrow," he growls, "and I'll kill you anyway. I may be just a human with extra pigment, but I'm from Chicago."

That does the trick. Flit nods and looks very uncomfortable.

"Been Outside, have you?" I ask.

"Some," she agrees.

"There a lot of that going on?"

"More than there used to be. More than when you were a Ranger, Twitch Pony."

"Twitch Pony?" Mike laughs.

I scowl at him.

"Like *My Little Pony?*"

"Shush," I tell him. "You're interfering." It's one thing to be called my full and formal name by one of Mab's other children. It's something else to be compared to a little girl's toy by one of the guys in the band.

"Do you have a brush for your tail, Twitch Pony?" He laughs more. It's annoying, and I try to look stern. "Or sparkles on your bum under that leather?"

"What do you want, Mike?" I ask him.

Mike stops laughing. "You know what I want."

"Right." I nod. "*Mike* it is. No more *Mikey*."

Mike nods, and the grin vanishes from his face. He points his shooter at Flit Fox and pulls back the part on top to make it ready. This probably doesn't impress Flit nearly as much as the cold iron at her throat, but he doesn't know that. He's trying to do his part. "Now tell the lady what she wants to know."

"Yes," I agree, and turn my stern face back to Flit. "What are you doing out there?" I ask.

"Scouting," she says. "Gathering information Mab and Oberon want. Following orders, which was never your strong point, Pony."

"Some might say that's because I bred true," I point out.

Eddie slams his fist into the wall, startling me and Flit both. "Jim!" he barks. "Where's Jim?"

"The Baobab Tree!" Flit splutters.

"Well, of course they're taking him to the Baobab Tree!" I snort my derision, as if it couldn't have been any other way. "But why?"

Flit glares back at me, sullen.

Eddie stabs her. It's just a little stab, a poke in the cheek, but Flit screams horribly. I smell the stink of death, like burning trees, and smoke hisses from the wound.

"*Cagado*," Mike says. He's shocked, and lowers the point of his shooter.

Eddie may be shocked, but doesn't show it. "Answer the question," he snarls, "or I poke this all the way through into your brain."

Of course Flit Fox's brain won't be anywhere so obvious as behind her face, but Eddie doesn't know that. And the iron hurts Flit enough that she takes him seriously.

"Belial!" she yelps.

I feel queasy. "What?" I ask.

"Belial wants him!" She's screaming her answer through tears, and Eddie eases off a bit, takes the blade out of her flesh.

"Him?" I ask. "Or the thing he's carrying?"

"Both!" Flit sobs. "Either! We've been watching for Jacob bar Azazel or for his father's hoof for many shifts! Mab said it would be soon!"

"Jacob bar Azazel?" Mike scratches his head.

"Jim," I tell him.

"Yeah, I get that it's Jim," he says. "I just wish the world would hold still for a second so I can focus on it."

"What's the urgency?" I ask. "What's the rush? Why does it seem like every power in the universe is dogpiling on us all at once?"

But Flit only cries.

"I don't know what to do with you, Flit Fox," I muse. "If I let you go, you're duty-bound to run off and tell Mab and Oberon we're here, and what you've told us."

Flit cries some more.

"You can't even promise me you won't, because you've already made a big deal about how good you are at following orders."

I'm genuinely a bit flummoxed.

"I could kill you, I suppose," I say, as if it was no big deal. It is a big deal. It's a big deal because I'm already permanently in trouble with Mab, and it's a big deal because I don't really like hurting my own kind. Especially here. It's one thing to fight the Rangers in the Outer Bounds when they attack me, but it's something entirely different to enter the Queendom and kill one in cold blood. This is my home. I can't do that to my home.

"I have an idea." The voice is Adrian's. I turn and see that the wizard is awake. He's standing up carefully, leaning against the wall and keeping away from the edge of the rooftop. "I mean, loose lips sink, and all that, but I think I could keep our friend's mouth shut as long as we need it to be."

He holds up the Eye.

Flit gasps. "Rahab!" she hisses.

Adrian chuckles. "Worse than that," he swaggers. "I'm gonna go all Vulcan on you."

He kneels over Flit Fox, who doesn't resist.

"Why waste a firebolt?" I ask. "We can just stab her."

"Not that kind of Vulcan." Adrian presses his hand on Flit Fox's face, with his pinky upside her nose and one finger at the corner of her eye. Flit's nervous, and she flickers in and out of showing fox as he does it, but the knife at her cheek keeps her still.

Adrian takes a piece of chalk from his pocket and draws lines around his own hand on Flit's face, including a circle around her mouth. "*Per Thoth te ad silentiam adiuro,*" he mutters. He plucks a bit of hair from Flit's tail, and then he backs off.

"That's it?" I ask. He hasn't fallen asleep or anything.

"That's it," he says, and puts the Eye back in his pocket. He carries that thing around like it's a cigarette lighter. He has no idea what it is. I'm not comfortable with my guesses, but unlike Flit Fox, I keep them to myself.

"Talk!" Eddie snaps, and pokes Flit again with the iron.

Smoke sizzles from her cut cheek, she hisses. Her mouth opens and shuts, but she doesn't say anything. She can't.

Mike holsters his shooter. "Look, I don't want to give anybody ideas, but won't she just write down what happened?"

"Fairies can't read." Adrian smirks at me.

I smirk back at him. "Fairies choose not to. Books are overrated."

"Either way," Eddie growls, "what do I do with this one?"

"Throw her over," I say.

Eddie doesn't hesitate. He drags Flit off the tiles. She scrabbles at him with vulpine paws, but he ignores her, and then he hurls her out into space. She falls, snapping her teeth mutely and showing fox. Serpents on the branches bite at her, and she looks like she's going to plunge to her doom on the forest floor below.

But she's not so disoriented as all that. As a snake the size of a cow unhinges its jaw to snap her up, she suddenly shows swallow. A single flap of her wings and she avoids the bite, and then Flit Fox goes winging off into the forest.

"What happens when they break the spell?" Eddie asks.

Adrian shakes his head. "Fairies can't do magic. Not like humans."

"Let me rephrase that," Eddie says. His voice is harsh. "What happens when you fall asleep?"

Adrian grins sheepishly. "Hey, I thought of that." He holds up the hairs from Flit Fox's tail. "We're covered. Just don't lose these."

"We'll be fine," I say. I don't know if it's true or not.

Eddie nods. "Have another stick of gum," he recommends. Adrian takes two.

"Which one is Belial?" Mike asks. "Is he the one with the cow head?"

"No." I remember Belial clearly. "He looks more like a squid. Or a mass of kelp. Or Jell-O with asparagus in it, like they eat in Utah."

"They eat Jell-O with asparagus in it in Utah? *Mierda.*"

"Stay focused," Eddie grunts. "How do we get to the Baobab Tree to rescue Jim?"

"We have a stop to make first," I say. "There's something we'll need."

"What kind of a something?" Eddie is suspicious.

"Think of it as a friend," I say casually. I really hope Pulse is where I left him. "Or a witness."

"We get this friend," Eddie thinks it out, "and the friend helps us rescue Jim. And then we go to the road Jim wanted to take us to."

I nod.

"And you don't want to tell me anything else about this friend, do you?"

I hesitate. "It'll be easier to show you."

"And how do we get to him?" Mike wants to know. "Or … her."

"Easy," I tell him. "But first we have to get down."

I show falcon and strafe down along the nearest tree branches climbing up over the rooftop. A scaled viper with long ridges on the top of its head snaps at me, but that's a mistake— I'm a bird of prey, and I eat snakes. I snatch the viper from the branch and hurl it down into the thorns below. A second viper meets a similar fate at my talons, and when a constrictor with stubby vestigial legs tries to coil about me, I show boy and pound it into senselessness with my fighting sticks.

"This way!" I call to the band.

Adrian comes first, followed by Mike, then Eddie in the rear, his boomer dangling ready by a shoulder strap and Jim's sword shoved through a slit in Eddie's jacket to improvise a sort of hanger for it. They're all deliberately not looking at the sky, and I realize that they're not used to anything other than plain, boring blue.

Adrian is a little shaky as he moves. It's not just magic that makes him conk out, I remember. It's pressure. I show him a pretty girl, nonthreatening. "Come on, friend," I say to him. "This is easy. It's a sidewalk."

It isn't a sidewalk, it's one branch under his feet and another clenched in his fists. But it isn't bad, and he takes a few deep breaths and then gets over it. By the time he reaches the thick crotch of the tree, he looks reasonably comfortable.

Mike follows, then Eddie. Say what you will about this ragged band of rock and rollers, we aren't cowards. And we aren't afraid of heights.

I lead the way again, scaring off more snakes, and also a pack of things that look like squirrels but have long fangs. Not Wild Things, just part of the Queendom, like the snakes. Halfway down the trunk, I plunge into the thicket. The thorns are tall here, they groan and they rustle a lot.

At the bottom of the tree, I show girl and look up. The last twenty feet or so of trunk are a bare slide to the ground, but the guys are hesitating well above that. I show falcon and fly up to them. They're all poised just above the top of the brambles, and I perch on the thorn bush branch nearest them and show reassuring, cheerful girl.

"Are you stuck?" I ask.

Adrian's eyes are closed, and he's breathing carefully. Mike Bass clutches his body tightly to a tree limb with one arm and with the other points to the bramble branch beside me.

I look. There's a body impaled on the bramble beside me. Thorns protrude from its chest, and hands stretch in my direction, pleading. The hands are frozen, but the corpse's white mouth works mechanically, opening and shutting.

"Hilarious," I tell them, and laugh.

They don't look amused.

"What?" I say, and I wave at the corpse dismissively. "If this showed up at your doorstep on Halloween, you'd tell it how cute it was and give it candy. Come on, Adrian. You've seen worse than this." I show him stern teacher, his secret crush, and then I drop to the ground.

They follow, mostly with eyes open.

Eddie drops to the thicket floor last, and when he stands, he looks around at the corpses impaled on thorns at every hand, their blood slowly dripping to the ground. "Twitch," he says, "I can't imagine why you would ever want to come back here."

"Home is where you ..." Adrian sniffs and nods. "Whatever."

"I've been to *your* home," Mike snorts. The big guy shudders.

"Well," I laugh lightly, "it's what you're used to, I guess."

Chapter Four

"How far are we from this friend, exactly?"

Eddie is the only one who can bring himself to look up at the corpses. I suppose this is the sort of thing he's used to seeing all the time, or at least whatever he sees out of that bad eye of his lets him shake this off without too much effort.

I don't take it seriously, of course. It's what the Queendom is showing here and now. It will show us other things later.

"That's not really the right question," I say. I'm almost running but not making much headway. The thorns around me seem to always be the same thorns, the caterpillars creeping away into the darkness under leaves bigger than my body the same caterpillars. The Push is strong on me, and it always presses into my face.

I have to stop for a moment, and I lean against Mike Bass. It helps, and to thank and entertain him for letting me lean, I show him pretty girl. He clears his throat and fidgets. I almost laugh, but I don't.

"Tell me the right question, then." Eddie grips his boomer in both hands. His eye slides sideways, and he grinds his teeth. "I can accept that I'm chasing after somebody's imaginary friend 'cause I've done things that were a lot weirder, but it still ain't my idea of fun. It'd get a little easier if I could at least understand why it feels like I'm running in circles."

"There aren't that many fixed places in the Queendom," I explain. It's painful to be so clear and direct, but I think we need Eddie to hold us together, and it isn't good that Eddie is asking hard questions. "Places that hold still, if you know what I mean. Getting from one to the other isn't so much a matter of following a road or taking a direction as it is a question of knowing where you're going and choosing to get there." There. I've practically told him everything. "And Pulse isn't imaginary. He isn't even properly dead."

"So you don't know where you're going?" Mike guesses. He looks at me, careful not to look around at the thorns. He shakes a little bit. I don't think it's the corpses that bother him. It's the fact that the corpses move and try to get his attention.

"Do you really think that's possible?" I sigh. The burden of having to share is painful. "Something's holding me back."

"What about that?" he asks, and points at a crumbling stone pagoda off in the trees. "Is that a landmark? Or might there be a road there?"

"It's just a remnant," I say, and when they all look confused, I sigh. "It's a piece of an older world," I tell them. "A bit of a ruin. There's lots of that stuff in the Queendom. Some of it is … is creatures, living things. What we call the Wild Things. But all of it moves. It isn't a landmark, no."

"What do you mean, *older world?*" Eddie squints suspiciously at the pagoda.

"I don't know what I *mean*," I tell him. "I just know what I *said*."

Adrian looks at me through the Eye. "The thing that's holding you back. Does it feel like a hand?" he asks.

"Yes," I say. Why not? "It feels like a hand holding me back."

"It looks like a hand."

"Thank you."

Eddie frowns. "What is it?"

"It's my banishment," I explain. I am humiliated. "It's a physical force, is what it feels like, pushing on me."

"Does it hurt?" Mike asks.

"Am I crying?" I counter. "No, it doesn't hurt. But it pushes me outward. I try to move in, and it holds me in place." I sigh again. "I think that's why we're not making any forward progress."

Mike leans in and whispers. "Can you trick it?"

"What?"

"You know," he continues, "pretend you're going the other way and make it push you where you want to go."

I snort. I'm tempted to show pony and kick him for that. "It's not a person," I tell him. "It's a decree. There's no tricking it."

"There doesn't appear to be any moving forward, either," Eddie adds.

Adrian is still squinting through the Eye, but he's looking past me now, over my shoulder. "I think I can help," he says.

"Oh?" I ask. "You see a path around my banishment through that, do you?"

The wizard shakes his head. "I see a lot of things, though. Tell me what you're looking for, and I'll try to get us there."

"It's a shack," I tell him. "It looks like a skull, and the fence around it is made of gravestones." I hesitate a moment, then add more. "It's a remnant, too, so it moves. Really, most things in the Queendom move around."

Adrian rotates slowly about me. He reminds me of a surveyor, or an artist examining a model. I hold still while he looks past me.

"I can see it," he says finally. "A woman lives there, or an ogre hag. She's big as a truck, talks like a child."

"Buzzard Betsy."

"She's carrying a doll."

My feet feel chilly with excitement. "Yes." That's Pulse.

Adrian pauses. "Eats children."

"Yes, that's Betsy," I agree.

"*Huevos.*"

Eddie pumps his boomer. It's a reflex. "Nice family you have."

"She's not one of Mab's subjects," I protest, "and she's definitely not family. She's just here." *And she's kind of funny*, I want to say, only I don't. "She's a bit of an older world too. I think she might have been a queen in her own right, somewhere, some time."

"I bet that was a great place to live," Mike mutters.

"The hand is pushing against you strongest from that direction," Adrian reports.

"Thanks," I say. "Your Eye is so mighty." I say it sarcastically, but in fact the Eye might be far more powerful than he knows.

"I think I can pull it aside." Adrian schemes. "For just a moment. What do we all need to do, just follow you?"

"Yes," I agree. "But how long is a moment? What if you fall asleep?"

"I'll carry him," Mike Bass offers.

I shake my head. "It was a stupid question. I'll carry him."

I show pony, and Adrian climbs onto my back. Mike and Eddie stand to either side of me, bending their knees like runners. They look silly, especially Mike. He's too big to look dignified doing much of anything except firing his shooter and playing bass.

"Ready?" Adrian asks. He's still looking through the Eye. His face is a little pallid.

I neigh. *Yes.*

"*Per … per Mercurium …*"

Adrian weaves on my back. Mike comes out of his starting crouch long enough to pinch the wizard.

"*Per Mercurium manum distraho.*"

I feel Adrian collapse, but at the same moment I also feel the Push disappear. It doesn't go away, it lunges past me, like I've suddenly become slippery.

I take advantage of the moment and bolt forward. The Queendom tries to show me thicker brambles and corpses that grab my ankles, but I ignore it and show it clever pony, dodging and dancing among the obstacles. I clatter over a fragment of road, hoping it doesn't distract Mike. The stones are worn almost to film, it's obviously just another remnant and doesn't go anywhere.

"Shiiiiiiiiiiiiit!" Eddie swings at obstacles with his boomer, but he doesn't fall behind, and no one takes the wrong road.

And then the brambles and the bodies are gone. We're at the edge of a clearing, and the sky again dazzles me with its many shimmering colors.

I stop at the row of headstones, show girl, and toss Adrian to the ground. He hits harder than I mean him to. I should be grateful, even though it's a little annoying that he basically forced me to admit to everyone that I'm subject to the Push. Okay, I am grateful. I crouch over him and pat his cheeks. He only meant well, poor boy, and he's knocked himself out again for the rest of us.

Eddie and Mike crouch too. They look around, boomer and shooter ready.

"Adrian, wake up." I show the wizard a picnic, with a stream and a basket.

Hyoo-hyoo-hyoo-waaaaoooo!

Hyoo-hyoo-hyoo-waaaaoooo! call the Mockers.

"What the hell is that?" Eddie asks.

"It's Adrian. He wakes up better if I'm gentle."

"No." Eddie points with his boomer at the trees surrounding Betsy's shack. I look and see that they're massive old oaks, bent over under the weight of their own dignity and trailing green evening gowns of Spanish moss. I hear them sharing secrets with each other. I can't hear the words, but the trees' voices are bitter and unkind. "What's *that*?"

"Trees?" I suggest, and then I hear the birdsong again. "Oh, *that*. Those are Mockers. They're imitators, like parrots or doppelgangers. They're Betsy's creatures, sort of her children. Come on, bonny boy."

"They sound like screaming kids." Mike shudders.

"Yes," I agree.

"Tell me this isn't your friend." Eddie looks like he wants to hit me. His eye is going crazy.

Adrian sits up. He's dazed, but I help him to his feet, and he can stand.

"This isn't my friend," I agree. "This is a violent monster. She isn't Mab's friend, either. She isn't anyone's friend. She's here because after Herself was chained, all the bits of the old worlds washed up here, ruins and reavers alike. Mab's folk leave her alone, which is exactly why I hid … my friend here."

Eddie's eyes narrow, impatient. "This is the friend who will help us get Jim out of the Baobab Tree. You hid him in the lair of a violent monster, the child-murdering queen of an older world."

"Yes," I say. It's more fun not to tell him everything I'm thinking. And his summary is basically true. At least, I hope it is.

"Lead on," Adrian mutters, "et cetera."

"Macduff," Mike volunteers.

"Actually," I say, "it's, 'lay on, Macduff, and damned be him who first cries "Hold! Enough!"'"

"You know your Shakespeare," Eddie says. It's not quite a compliment.

"I knew the man." That was well before I was Outcast, before humans started filling the Outside with all their machinery and Mab had to respond by constructing the Outer Bounds. In the Bard's day, mortals were more frequently guests in Mab's Queendom. There wasn't much of a boundary, back then.

"Well, I'm damned to start with," Eddie reminds me, "but lay on anyway."

I turn my attention to the shack.

It looks like a moldering boulder, moss and black decay like rot covering a heap of cracked stone with a thin gray-green film. One cavity, facing slightly away from us, is a window but looks like an eye. A second, pointing straight at us, is a door and a nasal cavity at the same time. A third hole, like another eye, faces skyward. Lazy, greasy smoke rises from it.

"I don't see her," I say. The fire makes me nervous.

Adrian pulls out his lens again and peers through it. "Nothing," he confirms. "What about the friend? What am I looking for?"

"I don't know how Rahab would see the doll," I tell him, and I hop the fence.

"What?"

The others hesitate, then follow me.

I want to be quick. Funny as she can be, Buzzard Betsy is a dangerous, destructive creature. She's not a queen anymore, but she's still a monster.

The grass in the yard is wiry and tough. Beetles scuttle across hard-packed earth, gnawing at the tough yellowish stumps that pass for a lawn. As I approach the hut, I hear a soft *bawk-bawk-bawk*.

"Oh," I remember to say. "Don't let the chickens bite you."

"Ow!" Mike hollers at that instant.

"Sorry!" I don't mean it. I also manage not to laugh, which is a good trick, since it's pretty funny.

Bang! Bang! Bang!

There is a moment of stunned silence. Mike Bass stands over the splattered bloody remains of one of the chickens. The others scatter for the far corners of the yard.

"Little *chingón* had teeth!" Mike looks shaken up and surprised. A chunk of fabric is torn from the ankle of his trousers, and he's bleeding.

"Hen's teeth." I grin. "Rare, those."

"Fangs!"

Hyoo-hyoo-hyoo-waaaaoooo! Bang! the Mockers take up the call. *Hyoo-hyoo-hyoo-waaaaoooo! Bang! Bang!*

"Oh, that's good," Eddie says. "That will help a lot." He scans the trees, and I think if he saw any of the Mockers, he'd shoot them. Fat lot of good that would do. They'd all just yell *boom* instead of *bang*, and the noise would be louder.

"Quick!" I vault in through the eye-socket window.

Crunch.

I land in bones. Not big bones like the shack is made of, but little bones. They're scattered all over the floor. As I land, a chicken scurries out through the front door, something clutched in her beak that might be a rib.

I want to laugh at this, because it's funny. But I can't, quite. And I don't know why.

Mike lands beside me with a louder *crunch*, and then Eddie Guitar.

"Hell, no," Eddie says, looking around at the bones. "Just … hell, no. How many damn kids … ?"

He's right. They look like children's bones, deep up to my ankles all over the bare dirt floor and in some corners drifting up to the height of my knees. Arm bones, leg bones, ribs, pelvises. No skulls. I smell rotting flesh, and I see gobbets of it scattered here and there among the bones, rotting so bad the chickens won't even touch it. Against one wall of the skull-shack is a heap of furs, and in the center is a smoldering pit of ash and coals.

"Tell me these are remnants of an older world," Eddie growls.

"They're remnants," I say softly. I'm lying. He doesn't believe me. "Funny, isn't it?" I don't quite believe myself.

Above it all, bolted into the ceiling with a nail that looks like a fragment of bone, hangs a cage. It's woven of twisted, thorny branches, and I guess from the size of it that it will probably hold two children.

"Son of a bitch," Adrian curses. He's come in through the door.

The Queendom isn't showing me bones, these are real. Buzzard Betsy ate the children whose bones these were.

I don't find that funny. Not anymore.

The other guys find it even less amusing. They all look sick and angry.

"Be grateful," I say. "When Rahab and the rider were defeated and thrown down into the sea from the First Mound, other things went with them. All the things meant to be excluded from mortal creation, and that included Buzzard Betsy. Bad she certainly is. She eats children and turns their skulls into her bird-creatures. Think how much worse she would be if she had free rein to come and go in your world."

"Let's get what we came for and get out of here," Adrian says. His eyes rove around like he can't bear to focus on anything.

"*Carajo*, yes." Mike starts digging into the furs of the sleeping pile. "What does your friend look like?"

"A rag doll," I say. "He has X's for eyes."

"What's a monster doing with a doll anyway?" Eddie asks. "Or is this just one more sign of how completely screwed up your native country is?"

"That's the easy question," Adrian says. "The better question is, 'Hey, Twitch, why are you friends with a doll?'"

"She hunts with it," I say. "It's a lure." Part of me wants to chuckle, and another part of me feels disgusted. "And Pulse hasn't always been a doll."

"Huh?" Mike is puzzled. He doesn't quite formulate a question, though, so I don't waste any time on an answer.

I show the falcon and swoop about the upper reaches of the room while Eddie digs into the bones. Adrian brings the Eye up and scans the room through it. His movements are stiff and forced.

There's no doll in the cage and nowhere else inside the shack to hide anything. And no Pulse, inside or outside his doll repository.

"Maybe she buried it?" Mike wonders.

"Maybe she lost it." Eddie looks angry.

"Maybe she ate it." Adrian looks bitter.

Hyoo-hyoo-hyoo-waaaaoooo! Bang! I hear a great flapping of wings in the oak trees outside, and I fly out through the eye socket in the ceiling. The Mockers storm this way and that through the trees. Something is disturbing them.

Or they're welcoming something home.

I drop to the roof of the shack and show girl. I'm on the lip of the opening, so I can peer down inside and see the guys scramble. They press themselves behind the wall and peek through the window to get a better look at the forest.

The flapping and crying noises reach a crescendo, and then an explosion of Mockers bursts from the trees. I found them funny once. Now the sight of them makes me want to cry out in objection. The Queendom isn't showing them, either. They're real. And they're horrible.

I hold my tongue for fear of what comes on their heels.

Mockers swarm about the bone shack. They shriek their all-too-human cries, some sounding like children weeping, some like children screaming. *No!* I hear, and *Please!* The Mockers whose cries sound like gunshots and birds are a relief.

I try not to look at them, but I can't avoid it. They swarm about me, press at me with gnarled and scaly claws. Their bodies might belong to eagles or large owls.

They have children's heads.

Only with no teeth.

I laughed at the Mockers on the day I first crept into Buzzard Betsy's shack to use her doll as a hiding place. I knew no Ranger would ever look there; Betsy was funny, but she was dangerous, and besides, Oberon likely hadn't told anyone exactly what I had. That would prove embarrassing. And Oberon himself wasn't going to go around knocking on the door of all the Queendom's worst monsters, asking after Pulse Lemur. I laughed at my cleverness, and I laughed at the silly bird-children and the chicken with teeth and at Betsy herself, because they were hilarious.

I'm not laughing anymore.

I can't say anything to the others below. Any word I utter will be repeated by the dozen bird-fiends clustered about me, scratching at me. Thank goodness for the leather clothing on my girl seeming, or I'd be bleeding badly by now.

I lean over the open hole to try to catch the eye of one of the guys, but pull my head back immediately.

Buzzard Betsy is coming out of the forest.

I quickly show falcon. My falcon doesn't look anything like the Mockers, who crowd around me *hyoo-hyoo-hyoo-waaaaooo-bang*-ing, but my girl, my boy, and my pony would fit in even less. I hop slowly on the top of the skull, claws scratching loudly at the bone beneath me, trying to stay behind the Mockers and at the same time keep an eye on Betsy.

She doesn't walk, she shambles. If there are legs moving beneath the rotting curtains that hang off her massive body, I can't see them. She wears a chain around her waist, which is something I don't remember. I smell blood and putrefaction, I see long nails and teeth filed to sharp, tiny points. I can almost feel the thick grease in the lank, knotted hair that hangs down

Betsy's back. I see eyes that glitter, wedged in tight above a nose like a twisted tree root. The nose comes first, snuffling and wheezing, but, big as it is, the biggest thing by far about Buzzard Betsy is her mouth. It's hinged at the back of her toad-like head, about where I imagine her ears ought to be, though I don't see any ears. It's lipless, the flesh at its edges ragged and raw, sometimes exposing gums and sometimes showing teeth, and it's so big that I think it could swallow me in one bite, even if I were showing pony.

I get a good, long look at Betsy as she oozes across her yard, scattering toothed chickens out of her path. I see the doll under her left arm, and I think about diving for it, but I can't. As Betsy bends at the knees and sluggishly climbs through the door of her shack, I smell her and I smell my own fear, and I see Eddie Guitar, Mike Bass, and Adrian Keys all scooting out the window at the same moment. They have guns in their hands and looks of panic on their faces, and they press themselves to the outside of the shack, staying out of Betsy's view.

I should snatch the doll and run, I think. With Oberon's help, I can free Jim and we can be gone.

Only I can't shake from my mind the vision of what I saw tucked under Buzzard Betsy's other arm as she marched across her yard. Maybe it's because my ears are still ringing a little from the shooting in the Outer Bounds, or maybe it's because I don't want to hear the noises that were coming out of their mouths, but in my mind's eye the vision is silent.

A vision of three children, kicking and screaming and unable to escape as Buzzard Betsy carries them into her lair.

CHAPTER FIVE

I slide down the roof of the shack to join Eddie, Mike, and Adrian. Landing hurts, and no wonder. I ache from exertion alone, not to mention the splinters in my rump and the cracks in my head from the ceiling of the Silver Eel. I'm such a mess, it's almost funny.

I point to the Mockers staring down at us from the roof and circling overhead, and I cover my lips with a finger. The last thing we need is all the Mockers crying out together in a chorus of, *So, Twitch, what's the plan now?*

Eddie nods. He's staring through slitted eyes.

Adrian points at himself and Mike Bass and at the door. Then he points at Eddie and the window, then at me and the hole in the ceiling. That sort of looks like the beginnings of a plan, but it needs a little work.

I point at myself and then make a gesture with my hands to describe the cage, hanging from the ceiling. They frown and shake their heads. Do they not understand, or do they disagree?

"No! Please!" one of the children inside the shack cries. It isn't funny. They're real, they're scared, and they need help.

Hyoo-hyoo-hyoo-no-please!

Hyoo-hyoo-hyoo-waaaaooooo, no-please!

Mike cradles nothing in his empty arms and rocks it to

sleep, then points at me.

I scratch my head, puzzled. Does he mean the doll, or the children? *Doll or children?* I mouth to him. He shakes his head back.

Eddie huffs, exasperated. He points at me and flaps his arms like wings. Yes, of course, I'm going to fly in through the ceiling, I get it, I can't very well burrow through it. But I don't know what they want me to do next.

Adrian kneels. He has a knife blade and he writes something in the dirt at his feet.

I try my best, but no amount of staring at the scratches allows me to read them. I shrug, flap my arms like wings, point at the ceiling and cradle an imaginary doll in my arms.

"Heeeeelp!" The scream is frantic, and the Mockers flurry about, agitated.

"Screw this!" Eddie pumps his boomer and walks to the door.

I spring into the air and show falcon. The Mockers pummel into me, the air is thick with them. A Mocker bites at my tail, but without teeth its bite can't hold me and I slip free.

Hyoo-hyoo-hyoo-screw-this!

Hyoo-hyoo-hyoo-waaaaoooo, screw-this!

Boom! Boom!

Through the flapping and writhing quasi-bird bodies about me, I can see the boomer's flash and smell its stink. He's hitting Mockers. I can hear their shrieks, and their agitation increases.

"Adrian!" Eddie shouts. "Can you clear these things out of the way?"

Then Mike begins to fire too. I can't see them very well, and I fight claw-to-claw to try to get free of the crowd. The Mockers butt into me and scratch me.

"*Aves repello!*" I hear Adrian shout.

That sounds like a good idea, I think, but only for a second. *Aves* means *birds*.

I'm a bird.

If I thought the Push was bad, the buffeting blow that whips off Adrian as he casts his spell makes it feel like nothing. I'm punched skyward along with all the Mockers. The rooftop of the shack and the yard around it are cleared of bird life out to a spherical perimeter marked at ground level by the tombstone fence. This means the chickens, too, and I almost laugh to see them hurled out like blown dandelion spores. They're so little, they keep sailing out past the fence and into the forest, and some of them get stuck in the Spanish moss. Chicken trees, that's funny, but I have to focus, and Adrian's spell is a problem.

The Mockers and I flap our wings and shriek in protest.

Hyoo-hyoo-hyoo-repello!

I can more or less watch the action unfold, forty feet directly below me. Adrian struggles at the window. He's holding up his candle and the Eye and trying to get off a spell, but he keeps catching himself against the side of the building. He's falling asleep.

Eddie advances into the shack, firing a blast off with his boomer at each step. Buzzard Betsy shrieks and flings aside the child in her hands, a girl in a nightdress. She bounces off the wall and hits the ground, still moving. Mike fires several bolts with his shooter and then he rushes in, running to grab the girl.

The other two children scream in the cage. I can't see Pulse.

I flap my wings but achieve nothing.

Adrian drags himself fully erect against the side of the house and gets off another spell. I don't hear the words over the shrieking of the Mockers and the gunfire, but I see the cage spring open. The children come spilling out, bony legs flapping pell-mell in all directions.

Mike grabs the girl at the side of the room and practically throws her out the window. Then he sees something and stops.

Betsy swoops down on Mike, jaws gaping. Eddie's boomer flashes fire into her side, but she ignores it, grabs Mike Bass, and clamps her vast mouth down around him.

Mike screams. It's a very high-pitched sound, considering how big Mike is. I laugh, but only a little.

Eddie lets his boomer drop to his side and pulls out his smaller weapon, a shooter like Mike's, only it can shoot very, very fast. He raises it, but Betsy snaps her head forward like a whip, spitting a projectile of Mike in Eddie Guitar's direction. Mike and Eddie collapse in a tangle of rock and roll musicians and lie still. There's blood. A lot of it.

"Oberon's beard!"

They need my help. The thought of the impact makes me nervous, but I show pony—

And fall.

Buzzard Betsy can't hear me coming, I guess, but the whistle of my own meteoric descent is huge in my ears. She shuffles a lurching step across the floor of her shack and bends to grab one of the unconscious men—

And I plow into the top of her head.

I choose to stay in equine form as I hit her, even though ponies aren't famously good at falling. But the pony weighs more than the boy or the girl, and things aren't looking good for my comrades. I take the impact more on my chest and forelegs than anywhere else, and Betsy and I are knocked flying in opposite directions.

I'm stunned, but I manage to show the girl, and I sort of roll once or twice before flopping to a complete, inert stop against the wall of the shack.

Lightning stabs me in the ribs. My right arm hurts, but I can't even feel the left one, and it dangles at my side, useless. Top to bottom—literally, since my head and my rump are both injured—I'm beaten and sore.

But I'm not defeated. I pull out one of my fighting sticks.

"Mab's belly button, Betsy," I say. "I hope that's enough for you."

Betsy makes a sound that's part groan and part roar. She's covered in those moldering drapes of a dress, so I can't see much in the way of detail, but I can tell that she's moving.

I roll over and somehow land on my knees. Then Adrian's at my side. He slaps himself in the face with one hand and with the other he drags me to my feet. "Easy, sweetheart," he says in a gentle laugh.

I laugh at him. "Are you using your Glamour on me, Adrian?"

"If the shoe fits," he says, "or something like that. Get the kids."

He grabs Mike and Eddie and starts shaking them. He's chanting something in Latin, and I hope it's a healing spell for Mike. I walk away, risking that Adrian falls asleep and all three of them get eaten by Betsy in so many gulps, but Adrian seems awake and motivated. Besides, I won't go far.

And someone should check on the children.

The three of them huddle against the tombstones. On the other side, a fluffy wall of angry chickens snaps at them with stolen children's teeth, and overhead, a storm of child-faced feathered ghouls variously yells *Bang! Boom! Repello!* and *Mab's belly button!* It sounds like an entire madhouse accusing me in court.

I show a kindly mother. This is not one of my natural showings, but it's one I've had to practice with Adrian from time to time, so it's one I'm quite good at. I limp, and I still can't move one of my arms, but they won't notice.

"Can you help us?" the biggest of the three children asks. She's a girl.

The middle child is a boy. His eyes are as big as coconuts, and he doesn't say anything. Clean streaks from tears cut through the dirt all over his face.

"Did you see the horsey?" asks the smallest child, also a boy. "A horsey came from heaven and saved us!" He shakes uncontrollably, and his eyes roll back in his head. If we get him home now, he'll probably start his own religion.

"This is all just a dream," I comfort him.

"We can't get past the chickens," says the girl.

"Bad chickens," I chide them, and I whack two or three of them aside with my fighting stick. They spit out bloody teeth and flap away. The others get even angrier, but they back down.

I gather the three children under my good arm and look back. Eddie stumbles in my direction, Mike leaning heavily across his shoulder. They're both bloody, especially Mike's shirt. Behind them comes Adrian. He's slower than Eddie, and I worry that maybe he's falling asleep, but when I see that he isn't, I realize that the truth is even worse.

Adrian is walking backward. He has his own shooter in his hand, and he's pointing it at the shack.

Graaaaaaack!

The ear-splitting cry comes from Buzzard Betsy. I know it from the tone, though I can't see her, and from the angered, violated sound of it.

And then I hear her footsteps.

"Run, children!" I push them towards the trees and begin laying about me with the fighting stick. I'd like to show pony and carry them, or show falcon and harass Buzzard Betsy, but I can't do either. As a pony, I'd be lame. As a bird, I'd be grounded.

Even showing boy, I only have one usable arm, and that one hurts.

But it's enough to beat a path through the chickens and the Mockers. The flying bird demons buffet me, but I stay hunched over, and they can't do much worse than that. Then I hear guns behind me.

B-rap-p-p-p-p! B-rap-p-p-p-p!

Mockers fall left and right, shredded by the bursts fired into their midst. The boomer goes off too, and then I plunge into the Spanish moss. It's cold and slimy, and I need a place to go or else I'll just run forever and Buzzard Betsy will surely catch me.

I aim for the Outer Bounds. I don't have to aim for any place in particular, since everywhere in the Outer Bounds is really the same place at the same time. It's all just out from the center. This time, the Push is at my back, and I fly. The others fly with me but not quite as fast, and I have to be careful not to leave them behind.

The Spanish moss slaps me in the face one last time, and then it's gone and I'm in a swamp. I hear shooting behind me still, so I don't think I've lost anyone. The swamp looks like it goes on forever, like the Queendom always does, and every ten feet is a new puddle of reeking slime. A row of Greek pillars and a half-submerged marble rooftop tease me with a moment of substance, but I know they're just a remnant.

Poking out of each puddle is a head. The heads are all talking to each other, *chatter-chatter-chatter-chatter*, none of it in any language I can recognize. It's probably not a real language anyway, it's just something the Queendom wants to show me.

I step into the first puddle with the children, and it's as deep as my neck. They go underwater.

"Dammit!" Eddie yells. "She won't stop!"

"I'm shooting for the eyes!" Mike shouts.

They both turn at the edge of the swamp and throw themselves behind a bloated log that lies half in and half out of the stew. I plunge into the cold, stinking water. I wish I had the use of both my arms. And I wish those heads would stop telling me jokes, so I could concentrate.

Chatter-chatter-chatter. A head framed in wispy orange hair grins at me from only a couple of feet away, lips peeling back to bare perfectly white teeth as I go under.

I find one of the kids and pull it up. It's the biggest, the girl, and I throw her onto her back behind Mike. He'll give her the most cover. My arm feels like it's about to snap in two as I toss her, and I see that Adrian's crouching beside the others.

And he's got the doll. Pulse.

So we just have to survive Buzzard Betsy, do something about the children, and then we can go spring Jim out of the Baobab Tree. No problem.

Overhead, the Mockers circle thick and dark. They've picked up the call of the hilarious heads now, and the air is thick with the sound of rattling teeth and soft, fleshy, gruesome imitation of the same, raining down from the sky. At least the Mockers can't really bite. I slap a water serpent gliding at me over the scum out of the way with one hand. Again I dive.

I grab another body, flailing, and I pull it out. It's the littlest kid, the visionary excited to see the falling horsey. He spits cold mud from his mouth, he's crying but he can breathe, so I think he'll be okay.

Mike is reloading and sees me; he grabs the kid and pulls him ashore.

"I thought you were dead!" I snap at him.

"Maybe I am!" The blood runs down his side and into his pants. While he's under cover, he pulls a flask from his pocket and drinks.

Eddie fires shot after shot into Buzzard Betsy with his boomer. I don't think they're seriously injuring her, but each shot forces her to stagger back a step or two, and they do leave purple blotches. As Eddie reloads, Adrian fires off a burst with his much smaller gun. It's sheer physical force that is holding the thing back.

"Hurry!" Eddie snaps at me, reloading his boomer. He doesn't tell me to leave the last kid. I dive.

I feel around in the cold mud, and for a moment I can't find anything. Then, fingers. I grab the hand and pull it up. This time it's me spitting out the mud, and when I pull the hand out—

I see it has no flesh on it. Just bones.

Wispy-haired Redhead smiles at me. "Chatter-chatter-chatter," he says, and his bony fingers squeeze mine.

"Oberon's buttocks!" I toss the hand aside.

Bang!

The head splatters. It was Mike Bass's shot. He nods at me, grimaces. "*Fundillo*," he says. "Get the kid." He turns around and shoots at Betsy.

Betsy's getting awfully close.

I feel like my one functional arm is almost detached from its socket, but I go under the mud again. It's cold and slimy, and that actually feels kind of good on my injuries. Especially the cuts on my head. When I feel body parts submerged in it, this time I check them for size. Wispy has an entire corpse under the surface, so it distracts me for a moment, but then I find the smaller body at its feet.

Smaller and still.

I grab the body and come back up. Filth streams off me and I hurl the boy to the bank. I fall to the ground next to him and the girl helps me. She pounds on the other child until he coughs and breathes again.

"Adrian!"

Mike kicks me with one foot and helps roll me over. I feel like a wet cat, and I resist the urge to shake myself and spray everyone. Instead, I run straight at Betsy.

"Twitch!" Eddie stops shooting and stands up from cover, exposing himself.

I jump straight for Buzzard Betsy's face. I raise my fighting stick as if the point is to hit her with it, puny little thing that it is.

Betsy's gray-green skin is mottled and veined even more than before. She looks like a bloodshot eyeball all over her body, with the red, ropy veins congregating in nexuses like bruises where, I guess, she's been shot. So she isn't having a very good day either. And she's pissed off.

Betsy grabs me with both hands. I'm expecting it, so the only surprise is how fast she is and how long her arms are. That's a big enough surprise.

She squeezes. I feel like all my ribs will shatter and my insides are going to burst. Maybe I've made a serious miscalculation. Betsy raises me to her mouth, her eyes glittering with rage and hunger, the raw flaps of skin around her mouth pearling her yellowish fangs with red.

I have a surprise for her.

I show pony.

Just for a second. I hurt even worse while showing pony than I do while showing boy, I feel like my chest is about to crack open. But in that second, just as Buzzard Betsy's face twists into a snarl of realization, I kick her right between the eyes.

Betsy goes down, and I show girl. I'm stronger when I show boy, but when I show girl I'm a little more resilient. And I roll better.

Still, the ground hits me like a humongous hammer.

Betsy makes a heavy gargling sound with a scream inside it. I feel like she's screaming for me, too, that's how bad it is. She clutches her face with her gigantic paws, and when she's able to get up, she'll be mad.

"The doll," I croak, and then clear my throat and try again. "The doll!"

Adrian heard me the first time, and he's already giving it to me. As soon as I hold it, I can feel Pulse. He jiggles a little bit inside. I wonder what it's been like for him. Not very comfortable, I guess, and he's had to see all the madness that Buzzard Betsy gets up to in her nasty shack.

Hopefully he's not too pissed to help me. I want Oberon to squirm.

"This way!" I cry. The direction doesn't really matter, but I pick a more cautious path, threading among the pools of muck and the babbling heads. I've put the fighting sticks away, and I carry the doll. Her misshapen mouth is funny, but it sort of disturbs me, so I turn her face to the ground and don't look.

The children follow me, then the others. Eddie is in the rear, saying hard words. Because he really wants me to believe him, he shoots one of the chattering heads just before we leave the swamp.

That's loud, but it doesn't matter. Betsy will know where we are because the Mockers are following us.

Hyoo-hyoo-hyoo-waaaaoo-boom!

Hyoo-hyoo-hyoo-waaaaoooo-graaaack!

We run through a field of tall grass, each strand as thick around as my finger and as stiff as wood. The meadow rattles as I crash through it, and I have to grab the middle child's hand to pull him through. The littlest fella has no problem and just charges straight ahead. A brook. A grove of pine trees on a hill, and we run down the other side.

And there's the wall, the Outer Bounds. It looms ahead of us, taller than anything, like it's actually holding up the glittering sky. And a gate. No Rangers in sight, but that's not so unusual. They'll be on patrol inside.

I push the children to Adrian. "Get them through the first mirror you can find that looks safer than here," I tell him.

"That shouldn't take long," he cracks, and puts away his shooter. "Come on, kids." He takes out the lens and squeezes it under his eyebrow as he drags the three of them into the Outer Bounds. They look at me with big eyes, like chipmunks, and then they're gone.

"Yell if you meet Rangers!" I call after him.

"I don't like your home, Twitch," Mike tells me. He's filthy and wounded, and he looks rattled. His breathing sounds like a bellows in need of oil and more than a few patches. I'm sure I'm no better, and I don't even have a good answer for him.

"Now what?" Eddie asks. "We aren't making progress."

"Aren't you the one in charge, Eddie?" I ask with my best innocent grin.

"Yeah," he says. "I order you to come up with a plan."

"I see. Okay, here it is."

Grrrraaaaaaaaack!

The wooden grass clatters, and a second later, Buzzard Betsy charges into view. She's even more mottled now because she's taken hits from the landscape as she's run through it, but she has a head of steam built up, and she doesn't stop. An unfortunate sapling in her way, my height and as thick around as my leg, explodes instantly into moist toothpicks as she charges through it.

"We take her down," I say. It's a joke, but they don't laugh.

"*Chingado.*" Mike sags, dropping to his knees.

Adrian emerges from the gate as Betsy rushes down upon us. He has the Eye in his hand, and he grins.

"I knew you guys would get into trouble without me." He laughs, squints through the Eye, and raises a stub of candle that he always carries in his pocket.

"*Per Volcanum …*" He yawns.

Betsy barrels closer.

Mike slaps his hands at Adrian, tries to pinch the wizard.

"*Per Volcanum ignem … Per … Per …*" Adrian sways on his feet.

Boom! Boom! Eddie fires shots at Betsy, but she's coming downhill at us now, she's mad, and the boomer isn't strong enough to knock her off her chosen path.

"You can do this, boyfriend," I whisper to Adrian, and I show him confident girl. It isn't easy showing him that, with my arm gimped at my side, my ribs most likely shattered, and my head nearly caved in.

Adrian nods. "*Per Volcanum—*"

He's still awake, but he can't get out the words.
"*Ignem mitto*!" I shout. Not a spark.
Buzzard Betsy is upon us.

CHAPTER SIX

aybe your friend can help!" Eddie snaps.

He fires over and over with his boomer. The empty shells from his weapon spin out into the air and rain around me. Mike fires too, but I think he's missing every shot.

"Aim low!" Eddie shouts to the big guy.

We can't stop her. Can we get away?

"Adrian!" I tuck the doll under my arm and slap the wizard. I'd shake him, but it would hurt my ribs too much.

"Volcanus ..." He rubs his face with his hands. He's struggling.

"Forget the firebolt!" I cry. "Let's get out of here!"

He perks up a little. "Leave the Queendom?" he asks.

"Abandon Jim?" Eddie barks. "No way!" He fires again.

"No!" Betsy rushes down the hill as fast as an automobile. "We'll just come back in a different way!"

Eddie slams out the last of his boomer shells, and it looks like he finally hits Buzzard Betsy's feet. She collapses, slamming into the moist earth like a bomb. Dirt flies up in all directions, and she plows a furrow wide and deep enough to plant hippopotami inside it.

"Ha!" Mike lurches forward onto his hand and empties his shooter into Betsy's back as she rumbles to a halt.

Eddie grimaces and pushes more shells into the boomer. The sword still dangles from his torn jacket. It looks wrong on him. "Maybe we don't need to run," he suggests.

Betsy raises her head. She spits mud from her quadruple-wide maw, vomiting out a croak as loud as thunder.

"*Huevos!*" Mike falls to his side.

"Into the Outer Bounds!" I shout, and I back through the gate. Mike tries to stand, his face twisted.

"Turn my head!" says a voice. It takes me a moment to recognize it. "I can't see all the fun!"

Adrian hears it too, and stares. He puts the Eye over his face and stares closely at the doll. Mike staggers towards me, reloading his shooter. Eddie steps deliberately, shooting all the while.

I hold the doll up and point the X's on her face towards Betsy.

"Oh, yeah," Pulse chuckles. "You're in for it now."

"Unhelpful git," I call him.

"Where's your sense of humor?" he chides me.

Betsy lurches to her feet, springing out of the furrow her vast bulk has dug in the earth. She lands with her legs wide apart and her arms spread. The nails on her fingers shine, greasy and ragged, and they look like they're all pointing my direction.

"Dammit," Eddie grumbles. "I coulda sold cars for a living."

But Betsy doesn't attack. She hangs in the air and quivers. Her beady eyes glitter and her jaw works, snapping open and shut and spraying fetid slobber each time. The Mockers above her circle and cry out.

"Here's one!" Adrian calls from behind me. "Opens into an empty restroom!"

And Betsy turns and shambles off. Her pace is strange, different from the shamble we've seen from her before. She seems to pull back with her shoulders, like the upper part of her is resisting something, and she leads with her vast belly. Her steps are ragged and irregular.

She's being pulled, is what it looks like.

Eddie raises his boomer to fire at her again, but doesn't.

"Son of a bitch," Adrian says.

"Chicken!" Pulse yells. "Come back here, you coward!"

Betsy turns her head and growls wordlessly at us, but she pushes through a stand of pine trees and is gone. The Mockers linger a few moments longer than their mistress, spitting bitter blame upon us.

Hyoo-hyoo-hyoo-waaaaoooo!

Then they, too, disappear.

"Booooooooooring!" Pulse howls.

Eddie pumps his boomer and presses the firing end of it to the doll's forehead. "I haven't known you long," he snaps, "but I think I can already tell how I feel about you."

"Ah," Pulse purrs. "This one's funny, Pony. No wonder you stayed away so long."

"I stayed away so long," I remind him, "because I was thrown out of the Queendom."

Eddie lowers his gun. All three of the rock and rollers stare.

"Did you say you put the kids in a restroom?" I ask Adrian. My head is spinning a little.

He shakes his head. "A daycare center. I'm not sure, but I think it might have been in Texas."

Eddie takes a roll of white tape from one of his packets and commandeers Mike's flask. He goes to work on Mike's injury, sloshing it with whisky and then bandaging it. Eddie was a soldier. He knows what he's doing.

Mike leans against stone and submits to being treated. "Why doesn't it have a tail?" he gasps. "Don't you all have tails?"

Pulse cackles. "Listen to the big Outsider!" he jeers. "He thinks I'm Pulse Dolly!"

"You are," I tell him. "The rest of you is barbecue."

"And I was such a handsome lemur," Pulse laments. He sighs. This is just a sound, of course. The doll isn't Pulse's body and doesn't move at all. "You could have taken me with you, you know."

"And carry a child's doll around with me everywhere I went?" I ask. "Or a skull?"

"You're already carrying a tail everywhere," Pulse points out. "How much worse would a doll be?"

"Worse," I insist.

The guys scratch their heads and make dubious faces at each other.

"That's not the real reason, though, is it?" Pulse Lemur never was a fool. No matter how stupid some of the things he did were. There's no point lying to him.

"I needed you to be hidden," I agree. "You were my insurance. *Our* insurance."

"Oberon was going to kill you!" Pulse's cackle sounds worse coming out of the doll's head.

"He was," I say. "Until I told him that killing me wouldn't save him. If he killed me, you would tell everything and he'd still be in trouble. Then he agreed to make me an Outcast instead."

"This is really charming," Eddie butts in. "Would you care to explain?"

I sigh, but Pulse leaps right in.

"Once upon a time," he says, "there were three friends. Hilarious, slap-each-other-on-the-back friends, all of them Rangers and one of them a King."

"Oberon," Adrian says.

"Shush!" Pulse says. "And these friends, they did things together that were truly funny. Fires and droughts and plagues and all the best things to induce a good belly laugh."

"Ha, ha," Mike says slowly. He isn't laughing. "*Cagado.*" Eddie finishes with the tape and hands Mike back the flask. Mike drains what's left.

"And one day, the King tells his two friends that the Queen has a visitor. 'Oh, is it like that?' the friends laugh. 'No, it isn't like that,' he tells them, 'she has a fancy, important visitor from another court, they're scheming together big, schemy plots, and the King and his Rangers are supposed to arrange a parade and a chariot.'"

"Belial." Adrian remembers.

"Belial, very good, one of the biggest Princes of Hell, sits right on the Infernal Council, and he needs a ride because his own beasties don't travel so well in the Queendom."

"Because of the light," Mike guesses.

"Because of the light," I tell him. "Some of the folk of Hell take it fine. Others are burned at the touch, like the Baal Zavuv."

"Stop interrupting me, Pony!" Pulse snaps. The doll's smile is fixed and greasy. "So these three friends plan a little joke, and it's going to be a good one because the more people who are upset and the more important those people are, the funnier the joke. The chariot's going to be pulled by six white horses. Or ponies. And the King doesn't have but the one shape, but his two friends can both show horse."

"Pony," I say softly.

"I thought you said you were a lemur," Adrian interrupts. "Isn't that like a monkey? Or a raccoon?"

"I can show a lemur," Pulse admits. "And also a big warhorse, a destrier."

"With a lemur's tail," Mike says.

"And proud of it."

"Not anymore," I remind him.

"I told you to stop interrupting. So the King and his two friends have access to the chariot and all the horses, you see? And they're Rangers, so they can move around in the Outer Bounds without anyone thinking anything about it. So the three of them make a quick trip through to the Outside, and they collect beans. Bushels of beans."

Mike snickers.

"Hell," Eddie curses. "You're like children."

"Beans, beans, the musical fruit," Adrian chuckles. "You know ..."

Eddie snorts. "I'm surrounded."

"And when the chariot team is eating, to get their strength up, an hour or so before the chariot ride, the friends make good and sure that the team eats lots and lots of beans. The friends tell them that it's special food, a reward for their special and very important duty. And the horses' stomachs aren't used to beans, naturally."

"Naturally," I say.

"Why not?" Mike asks.

"Because they're not Mexican fairies," Adrian sneers.

Mike looks annoyed. "Lots of people eat beans."

"Yes," I agree, "but not fairies. Beans are a human food, like maize or Twinkies. The Queendom doesn't have such innovations. Mab's subjects mostly eat fruit, nuts, and meat. Their bellies don't handle human food any better than human bellies can take the food of the Queendom."

Eddie laughs sourly. "You're all paleo."

Pulse laughs with audible glee. "We were paleo before there was a paleolithic! And so we meet him at the Crossroads and carry him across the Queendom, and right there, on the Avenue of Stones leading to the main gate of the Shadowless Palace, it happens."

"Trumpets," I say. I don't mean to, but I chuckle a bit. It's funny, after all.

"Trumpets!" Pulse yells. "Great blasting farts—and worse—from bellies unable to handle legumes, all aimed at blobby, tentacle-faced Belial, and the horses can't even turn away to be discreet about it because they're all in harness, and me and my friend Pony here right in the back, right in front of the Infernal, hooting away!"

He cackles. I laugh too. It's hilarious. I guess we laugh too long, because Eddie Guitar cuts us off.

"Then what?" he asks.

Pulse is silent for a moment. "Show him."

"You sure?"

Pulse says nothing. Then he snaps. "What? I nodded yes, didn't I?"

"No," I say, "you didn't nod. You can't nod anymore, remember?"

I pull apart the stitching at the back of the doll's head. It's tricky work with just one hand, but I do it, and then I reach inside and pull out stuffing so I can remove Pulse from his container. I toss the doll aside and hold up Pulse Lemur.

Pulse is just a skull. A smallish skull, like a child's, though a human scholar would puzzle over it, note its lemur-like snout and front teeth, and pronounce it a new species of pseudo-hominid, and congratulations to Charles Darwin. That funny old man gets credit for us all the time.

"*Carajo*," Mike says.

"What happened," Pulse continues, his jaw not moving at all as the sound of his voice clearly emanates from the bone, "is that Belial blasted me."

"Chaos," I add. "Everyone bolts, the chariot is overturned, Belial falls off the Avenue and kills a hundred people in his thrashing about."

Pulse laughs. "Unbelievably hilarious. The funniest day the Queendom has ever seen."

"And we get in trouble," I add.

"Two of us get in trouble," Pulse corrects me. "The two lowly Rangers. Or rather, the one, you, since you immediately rush me off and hide me in the shack of old Funnybones there."

"Sorry," I say.

Pulse giggles. "For what? I've been laughing nonstop since you left!" As if to demonstrate it, he cackles long and loud. The laugh bothers me, and it reminds me of the bones scattered on the floor of Buzzard Betsy's shack.

"Oberon blamed us," I say to the band. "He was going to have me executed, only he knew I had Pulse's skull, and he was afraid if he killed me, Pulse would tell."

"Which I would have," Pulse said, "because that would have been hilarious. Can you imagine how pissed off Mab would have been?"

"Only it was something of a bluff," I finish, "because Pulse was hidden, and no one ever would have heard from him again. But Oberon didn't know that, and we had a standoff, and we resolved it by him pleading with Mab to just exile me."

"That's serious." Pulse's voice sobers up. "No one's been exiled in a century or more. No wonder I haven't heard from you."

"None of this explains what good this skull is going to do us," Mike complains. He looks a little pale, but give him credit, he's on his feet.

"Sure it does," Eddie contradicts the bass player. "We're going to blackmail Oberon, the King of the fairies."

"You make it sound so tawdry," I object.

"I don't think it's tawdry," Pulse says. "I think it's very funny."

I'm not surprised.

"Unless anyone has a better idea … ?" I leave the possibility out there for a few seconds, but no one volunteers anything.

"Now's a great time to squeeze the little pimple," Pulse giggles.

"Yuck." Mike puts away his shooter.

"Really?" Adrian asks. "All we've been through, and the word *pimple* makes you uncomfortable?"

"I can think something is gross without feeling uncomfortable."

"In this band," Eddie says, "that's a necessary skill."

"Why is now a great time?" I ask. "What's going on?"

"Something big." Pulse's voice is animated.

"How do you know?" Eddie says. "You've been stuck inside a doll."

"Yeah. Why the doll anyway?" Mike asks.

"I knew that even if it occurred to anyone that Pulse might be hiding inside Betsy's doll," I say, "nobody would want to be the one to go and check." I consider, and without meaning to, I shake Pulse around in my hand.

"Hey!" he snaps.

I laugh. "Not so funny?"

"No, it was funny," he admits.

"So something's going on with Betsy." I think about that some more. "But Betsy's not the sort to make big plans. What's the chain about, then?"

"Got it in one!" Pulse hums. "But I don't know what the chain does."

"You must have seen who put it on her," Eddie says.

"Do you sleep?" Mike asks.

"A man in a funny hat," Pulse says.

Adrian grimaces. "Isn't that how *Curious George* starts?"

"That's the man in the yellow hat," Eddie reminds him. "I can tell you never had kids."

"Never really even *was* a kid," Adrian admits. The raw, dry sound in his voice reminds me of the children's bones on the floor of Betsy's shack, and I shudder.

"Funny how?" I ask. "Did the hat kill people?"

"Funny like out of place. Funny like a cowboy hat, only not really, and it has tails. Funny like in all the years I spent looking through mirrorgates at the Outside, I don't ever remember seeing a hat quite like this one."

"And it was a man," I repeat. "Not one of Mab's children."

"A man, and an old one."

"An old man in a funny hat." Eddie guffaws. "It isn't Curious George; it's Gandalf."

"And then what?" I ask. "Am I right to think the chain makes Betsy do things?"

"I still don't know," Pulse insists. "The man in the hat put that chain on her. Occasionally, out in the trees, Betsy runs into other Wild Things with chains on them."

"Wild Things?" Mike asks.

"Like Betsy. Monsters from before the Queendom. Things that don't bow the knee to Mab and are dangerous. And a lot of them have chains on now."

This news makes me feel uncomfortable, but it probably has nothing to do with us. "You sure it isn't Mab's doing?"

"How could I ever be sure of that?"

"Jim," Eddie reminds me. "A Baal Zavuv got Jim, remember?"

"We're going to the Baobab," I tell Pulse.

"You don't look like you're in any shape to do that," he points out.

"You can see too?" Mike asks.

"I have no choice," I tell the skull.

"That'll be fun, then." The skull doesn't move, Pulse can't move, but at this moment his teeth still give me the impression of a slightly insulting grin.

"Suddenly I'm not so anxious to go," Mike says.

"Adrian," I say, "I think I can get us to the Baobab if you can get me around the Push again."

"Easy as falling," Adrian says. "As they say."

"Everybody ready?"

Eddie pumps his boomer. Mike runs his fingers through his hair. Adrian squints through the Eye. I turn to face away from the Outer Bounds, and the stiffness and sharp pangs that lance through my body remind me that I'm hurt. Bad.

"Here we go."

I can't run, and I certainly can't show pony and gallop, but I jog as fast as I can manage. Adrian chants, and the Push slides off my body again.

We run over the top of the dune and through the pines, but now the other side of it is covered in desert. Mirages of camel trains, tents, and date palms fade in and out of my vision. Needle-thin, tree-tall columns of rune-speckled stone jut accusingly at the sky here and there across the dry landscape. Atop a mountain-high dune stands a giant with a serpent head, a kilt about his waist, and a huge curved scimitar in each hand. The ground is a red-hot iron pan, and it burns my feet. I ignore it like I ignore the man-tall cacti that sing at me, the carpets of scorpions slithering quietly under all the rocks, and the eyeless newts skittering over the sand, belching tumbleweeds. I ignore it, and then it's gone, replaced by grasslands, the grass of which is taller than me and the earth of which is covered in ice-cold water up to the middle of my calf.

Then that's gone too, and I stop running. I'm standing beside the Hedgerow, a thick, dark-green wall of ivy. The others step to ground beside me, and I show Adrian grateful girl.

"Well done," I tell him. I mean it. I hurt all over.

He grins. He looks totally awake. "No sweat."

Eddie and Mike examine our surroundings suspiciously. We're in a small forest glade, totally bounded on one side by the Hedgerow.

"Is it my imagination," I ask the sorcerer, "or is your curse getting easier?"

He shrugs. "Some, I guess. I feel like I'm working some things out."

"Holy crap," Mike mutters. He's pressed his face against the Hedgerow to peer through it. "Not *that* guy."

"Aha," Pulse says. "This is where things get really funny."

I press my face up to the Hedgerow to take a look.

CHAPTER SEVEN

The Baobab towers over everything within the Hedgerow, but I can barely see the great knobbly disks of its foliage, high overhead and parallel to the ground. What I see at first is an explosion of color.

Tents and flags. The biggest, fanciest tents are over by the tree. I can see the gold and purple cloth of their flaps and Rangers standing guard around some of them. Nearer the Hedgerow are plainer tents, and swarming around the tents are more of Mab's subjects. Throughout, there are tables laden with food—berries, haunches of meat, roasted squash.

"Don't even think about it, Mike," Eddie hisses.

"What?" Mike grumbles.

"I'd kill for a coffee myself," Eddie says, and spits on the ground. "But don't even think about it."

"Think about it, both of you," Pulse whispers. I tuck him away and out of sight so I'm the only one who can hear him finish his thought: "It'd be hilarious."

"I got a candy bar anyway," Mike says, and pulls snacks from the Silver Eel's green room out of his pockets. "Want one?"

Eddie shakes his head. "Too solid."

Adrian shakes his head. "Too heavy."

"Suit yourself." Mike munches on a bit of chocolate. He trembles a little as he eats it. He needs the energy, even aside from the fact that Betsy bit him.

The Mockers circulate among the tents, picking flesh off platters at the banquet tables with their toothless mouths. Their cries mix into a general cacophony that is muted by the thickness of the Hedgerow. I see Buzzard Betsy too. She stands in a trodden-down circle of earth, shifting slowly from one foot to the other and muttering.

And there are others, many of them. Crawlers with odd numbers of legs and gigantic, needle-filled mouths. Slitherers with heads at either end and tongues that drip saliva, each drop burning a smoking hole into the ground. Shamblers like Betsy, overgrown and moldering. A creature with six lizard-like legs, no tail, and a bobbing, wiggling lump of flesh hanging on an antenna in front of its mouth. The lump of flesh looks like a human baby. Bellowers, leapers, dancers, creepers. Every Wild Thing in the Queendom has been rounded up and stands around the Baobab. This is unnatural. They should be killing each other and killing Mab's children and running amok, but instead they fidget like children made to wait too long.

Every single one has a chain around its waist.

"Mab's knobby knees," I mutter.

"What is this?" Eddie asks.

"I can't be sure," I tell him. "But if I had to guess, I'd say it's a council of war."

And then I see the man Mike was talking about.

He sits at a table on a low rise close to the tree. Half the hill has been scalloped away, leaving a gentle slope terminating in a cliff. Seated around the table are various parties I know. I see Belial the Scabrous, the big tentacle-waving, scale-encrusted, semi-gelatinous Prince of Hell. Beside him is a Bearer of the Word I recognize, the whiny, treacherous archangel Raphael. They stand at the bottom of the cliff so they can participate at the level of the table despite being many times bigger than all the others. Around the table at the top of the hill, seated on carved wooden chairs, are Mab and Oberon and the man Mike noticed.

It's the man in the funny hat, the funny hat being a round-and flat-brimmed piece of red headgear with tassels behind it. He wears a red half cape, too, and I've seen him before. We saw him on top of a meatpacking plant in Dodge City, Kansas. I recognize the Legate of Heaven immediately, even without the four golems and the red palanquin resting at the bottom of the hill.

"Where's Jim?" Eddie asks.

"He's got to be inside the Baobab," I tell him. "You'll see him when we get closer."

Eddie is silent for a moment. "I just don't see how that can happen," he says. His voice sounds heavy, maybe heavier than it ever has before, which is saying something. Eddie is not a cheerful man.

I show him cute girl. Not too cute, I don't want to irritate him, just cheer him up a little. "Keep your chin up, darling," I tell him. "We'll think of something."

Eddie looks away.

"Oberon," Mike reminds me. "That's the plan, right?"

"And what else would it be?" I show Mike the same cute girl, and he looks flustered.

"I can get us inside," Adrian says. "A ward of seeming is no big deal."

"Easy for a sorcerer like you," I agree.

"But then what?" he asks.

"Can you make us look like Queen's Rangers?" I ask. "With leather jerkins and greaves and spears?" I encourage him by turning up the cute girl. "The tree and the lightning bolt?"

"Sure." He grins. He holds up three long hairs, and I remember that he took them from the tail of Flit Fox. "I can even give you a face Oberon will recognize."

I grin back. "And what will happen to the spell you put on her, sealing her mouth?"

Adrian shrugs. "There's a risk it goes away," he admits. "But do we have a choice? If you're going to walk up to that table, don't you need to be someone Mab and Oberon know and trust?"

"Do it!" I say.

"Oh, this will be good!" Pulse cackles, close against my body where no one else can hear him.

Adrian tucks the hairs into the pocket of my jacket.

"Copping a feel, cheeky boy?" I wink at him.

He chuckles and then marks each of us with a chalk glyph on our foreheads, including his own. He hesitates. "Pulse?" he asks.

I pat the bulge where I've tucked away my friend. "He'll stay with me."

"*Per Mercurium facies muto!*" he incants, and then we all look like Queen's Rangers. The others still have their own faces, though, or at least narrowed, tighter, smaller versions of their own faces. And Eddie looks like he's been bleached.

"How do I look?" I ask.

Adrian sways a bit on his feet, and I put my hand on him and show him sexy grin to strengthen him. He snaps out of his wooziness and winks at me.

"Like Flit Fox," Eddie says.

"Let's not waste it," I suggest.

"Lay on, Macduff."

You can't walk around the Hedgerow because it grows in a complete circle. It only has one gate, too, and that's far away around the perimeter, leading off to the Avenue of Stones. Besides, any self-respecting fairy wouldn't walk around to the door—she'd fly over the Hedgerow or climb through it.

We'll have to improvise.

"Eddie," I say, "do you have a knife?"

Of course Eddie has a knife. In two shakes, he's cut a pair of branches out of the Hedgerow, creating a narrow passage through it. I lead, keeping Adrian close behind me. Mike follows, and then Eddie brings up the rear. He looks like a small, elfin black man with all the color sucked out of him, holding a wooden spear. I'm pretty sure that under Adrian's ward of seeming, the spear is really Eddie's boomer.

We emerge from the Hedgerow behind a mud pit. In the mud, things shaped like worms and as big as horses roll over each other and gnaw each other's rubbery flanks with toothless mouths. They're chained, too. I've never seen such a sight as these chains on all the Wild Things, and I wonder what the chains do.

And why Mab is letting the Legate of Heaven go around in her Queendom, chaining up all the Wild Things. And why she and the Legate are sitting down to a picnic at the Baobab tree with Belial, the ugliest Prince of Hell.

I grin at a couple of Rangers standing a gluttonous watch over a trio of ostriches roasting on a spit.

"Flit Fox," they nod.

"Wiggle Emu," I nod back. I nod again to the other, whose name I don't know.

"Pony, you clever clogs, you," Pulse murmurs. "Wouldn't it be funny if I started yelling right now?"

"It would," I agree. "It'd be so funny, I'd have to smash you to tiny pieces on the spot, before I even tried to defend myself or get away. And that would be hilarious too."

"Yes, it would," Pulse agrees, but his enthusiasm is a little more muted.

I make a beeline. I look officious, like I have an important task. I can't very well go slinking around trying to avoid notice and then walk up to Mab's table, so I go bold as brass. Also, walking fast means no one invites me to eat and no one makes any serious effort to engage me in conversation. This ruse won't work if someone has just seen Flit and knows she's under a spell—or thinks Flit is missing in action and wants to ask me questions about it. I return waves and salutes and call out names when they occur to me.

Walking fast does hurt quite a bit more than walking slow, though. I try not to limp visibly. I probably fail.

We approach the bluff. I pass the corner of a boxy tent full of spears and leather greaves and stop a moment at the sight of the Baobab tree.

A baobab of any sort is a strange-looking tree, with a really thick trunk and a shallow canopy of branches arrayed at its top like a collection of lily pads on the surface of a pond, each lying parallel to the ground below. This baobab, *the* Baobab, is particularly strange. It has open woody knots all about its barrel chest, and the knots are stained with blood. Its roots part from its trunk ten feet above the earth and explode down like a skirt of wooden snakes, plunging into the ground only inches apart. The roots quiver when touched, and only part upon the command of Mab or Oberon. Which makes the space underneath the Baobab's trunk a sort of prison cell.

Jim stands in the cell, glaring out at the world.

"Look at that stubborn son of a bitch," Adrian says. He means it as a compliment. "If he only called for his dad, don't you think he'd be rescued in a heartbeat? But instead he just stands there wearing *pissed off* all over his face."

"That's rock and roll for you," Eddie says. "Arm up."

Eddie hands out spears from a dried elephant's foot like an umbrella stand. That's smart. I take one. Even if I can only use it with one arm, the thing has a sharp point on it, unworked enough that it will poke a hole through any of Mab's children.

"*Mierda*," Mike mutters. He's staring at the Baobab. "Is that thing a tree or a monster?"

"It's a tree," I say. "A tree that eats flesh and can move."

As if it's heard me, which it clearly hasn't, the Baobab's trunk shudders.

"Is it a … a Wild Thing?" Mike asks.

I cock my head and consider for a moment. "I don't know," I admit. "I think it's like Rahab. Old like the Wild Things, but sort of a special case. The tree doesn't wander around in the Queendom, it stays here. The Baobab serves Mab."

"This is nuts."

"True," I admit. I'm just glad the Baobab isn't wearing a chain around its trunk.

"Let me see!" Pulse hisses.

"Once." I take him out and give him a good long look.

"Hey!" he cracks as I stuff him back inside. "It's just about to get really good."

"Don't worry," I say, "you'll be in the thick of it."

"You going to bring Oberon over here, then?" Eddie asks.

I look around the edge of the clearing and nod a direction. "Get as close to the tree as you can without getting into trouble. I'll bring him to meet you."

Eddie pumps his boomer. It looks like he's holding two spears and stroking one of them. "What makes you worry I'd get into trouble?" he asks.

I show him a dazzling groupie, though I don't know how much of it he can see through Adrian's wards. "That's rock and roll for you," I tell him.

I leave them and walk up the hill. A few steps along, I am challenged by a sentry, but when I growl at him, he shows dormouse and backs down. I hear music playing over all the monstrous and bustling sounds of the council, and I see that on the far side of the bluff stands a little band, playing to entertain the table. There's a harpist, and also something that looks like a guitar but has a really long neck and only three strings, a pair of kettledrums, and a tambourine player. For a crazy moment, I want to walk away from my mad plan and simply sit down with the band and play.

Just for a moment, though. Then I get control of myself and focus on the table.

Mab is resplendent. She's tall and thin with hair like gold, and oak leaves ring her about the ears. Oberon looks like he's her match, like he might have hatched out of the same nut, even, same height and build, though his hair is jet black. But he's wrapped in that tailed coat and trousers that she chose for him, and he's got an expression on his face like a servant or a dancing monkey, eager to please. Mab's the one who wears the skirt in the family.

The Legate looks ageless, though he feels old, so old he can't be human, I think to myself. I don't look at him because when Mab and Oberon are entertaining others at their table, a Ranger would be careful not to molest the guests. I don't look at the Infernal or the Angelic, either, though they both practically scream at me, begging to be stared at. Belial looks like an octopus upside-down in bloody aspic, and he sounds like cars being torn apart with metal snips. Raphael burns white. There are meat and wine on the table in front of them, but no one appears to be eating.

I feel strange as I approach. I try not to think about my feelings, but they poke through anyway. Do I miss this place? Do I want to be here? This is my home, isn't it? Isn't this why I'm fighting to get Jim into Hell and force Azazel to do us favors—so Azazel will forgive any affront I caused to Infernal dignity and insist that Mab take me back?

But what is Belial doing here again? And with the Legate, a man who schemes against Hell in order to be able to scheme against Heaven?

Is my quest misguided to begin with?

"I want to see," Pulse mutters. I rap him on his bony forehead, and he shuts up.

Now is not the time to ponder and re-ponder.

I stop an appropriate distance from the table and bow. The Legate pauses in midsentence and waits. Oberon sees him waiting and turns to look at me.

"Yes, Fox?"

"My Lord," I say, "there is a disturbance in the Outer Bounds that may require your attention."

"Again?" Oberon rolls his eyes and climbs to his feet. "Pardon me, ma'am," he says to Mab, kisses her hand, and then flops in my direction. He's wearing the long, pointy-toed shoes of state to go with his formal tails, and they slap loud on the grass behind me as he follows me away from the table.

I feel a burning at my back, which might be the angel Raphael, or the Legate's stare, or worse.

"Far enough," Oberon whines, and flaps to a halt. "What is it, Fox?"

I want a little information before I tell him anything. "You heard about the scuffle?" I ask. I am careful to stand so that he is between me and the parties at the table. "The resistance put up by the Outsiders?"

"Yes," he says, and points to Jim. "The Baalim delivered bar Azazel to Belial, who turned him over to us. I'd heard you were missing, and I'm happy that isn't true."

I see Eddie, Adrian, and Mike. They're standing around a fire pit with Queen's Rangers, warming their hands and doing a credible job of looking like bored soldiers. They're not as close to the Baobab as I'd like, but they're within a short sprint.

Jim still glares out at the clearing.

"But you see, Obie," I tell my King, my one-time friend, and the First of the Queen's Rangers, "Flit Fox *is* missing."

I take Pulse out and hold him between us.

Comprehension slowly dawns on Oberon's face.

"Mab's shiny belly!" he hisses.

"Don't let her hear you say *that*," Pulse warns him.

"Well, I can't very well curse by *Oberon*, can I?" He glares at me.

"Why not?" I smile. "I do."

"Hello, Obie," Pulse says. "It's been a long time."

"How do you look like Flit Fox?" Oberon asks me. He stares close, at me and at the spear. "How are you showing me this?"

"It's a secret," I said. "Learned it in the Rangers!"

"Liar!" Pulse gasps.

"Not that I'm anxious to see you again," Oberon whispers. "Especially not here and now." He hops from one foot to the other, like he's about to show a crow. Which he can't do. Oberon can only ever show Oberon. Right now he's showing surprised, uncomfortable, edgy Oberon.

"Unfortunately," I tell him, "it isn't my choice. I need a favor from you, and I need it now. And in fact, I need it right here."

"When you say *favor* ..."

Pulse laughs.

"I mean that you're going to do what I tell you, or I'll march over there with my friend Pulse and we'll tell Mab and Belial exactly who was responsible for the Avenue of Stones." I smile flirtatious teeth at Oberon.

Oberon's pale face grows paler. I can see wheels spinning inside his head, and I wonder what they're churning. I take a guess.

"It looks to me like now might be a particularly bad time for this news," I say, looking over Oberon's shoulder at the table. "Mab getting all cozy with Belial like that, she might have to throw you overboard to stay on the tentacled fella's good side."

Oberon snarls. "What do you want?"

"My friend," I say, and as I say it I realize that I'm saying something important. Something true. I nod at Jim. "Jacob bar Azazel. Tell the Baobab to let him go."

He looks stunned.

"It can be discreet," I suggest. "Tell it to just part its tails ever so slightly in back, and Jim will be on his way and gone long before anyone realizes."

Oberon looks over his shoulder, making sure no one can hear us. "You're mad!"

"Yes, she is!" Pulse agrees. "And I'm bored. I haven't seen a child get eaten in ages. So let's quit this nonsense and get to it!"

"Get … get to what?"

"You choose, Obie," Pulse says. "Either way, you might make Mab really, really angry with you." He chuckles.

"Are you afraid of being caught?" I ask, and my own question makes me curious. "Can the Baobab tell on you?"

"Yes!" he snaps, then recovers himself. "The Baobab will tell Mab that I ordered the prisoner released."

I enjoy his squirming quite a bit, but I'm afraid it might be too hard for him. The end objective, after all, isn't to make Oberon uncomfortable, it's to get Jim out of confinement. "I'll make it easy," I say. "Tell her I tricked you. You saw Flit Fox, loyal Ranger, and he told you that a rescue attempt was going to be mounted on behalf of the prisoner Jacob bar Azazel. To prevent the rescue, you ordered Ranger Fox to move bar Azazel to the Shadowless Palace. You had no idea that Flit Fox was really the notorious Outcast Twitch Pony in disguise, and you're shocked to hear it."

Oberon hesitates. I think I've got him.

"Aw, that's no fun," Pulse complains. "What is there to laugh at if no one gets hurt?"

Then something scurries across the grass behind Oberon. It's quick and it's red and I try not to look at it, but I must glance at least briefly, because Oberon turns his head to see what's happening.

It's Flit Fox. He's running flat out for the table, and as Oberon and I look at him, he starts barking at the top of his lungs.

I bring up my spear, but I'm not fast enough. Oberon punches me in the jaw. The blow sends me reeling, and I drop Pulse onto the grass.

The skull laughs uproariously. "Now, *that's* hilarious!"

Chapter Eight

I lose my grip on the spear and roll through the grass. An enormous bellow rings off the shimmering vault of the sky from the hilltop, but I can't pay it any attention. I try to slither away, and Oberon picks up the spear.

He comes after me. He stabs for my head and misses, then for my chest and I roll aside. A third time he aims right at my belly, and I don't have time to move—

At the last second, I show falcon. The point of the spear rams down through the long silver hairs of my tail. It pulls hairs out, and that smarts, but I'm not injured.

I pull out one of my fighting sticks. Oberon rears up, spear raised over his head in both hands to thunder down upon me and impale me like a bug. His face is stormy, roiling and flashing lightning.

I throw the stick, and it hits him between the eyes.

Oberon falls back. "Mab's knuckles!" he howls, clapping long fingers over his face where I've pounded him.

I cast around for anything I can fight with and find Pulse.

"Ha ha ha ha ha!" he cackles. I don't find it very funny. "You've pegged him right in the nose, Pony! How does that feel, Obie, my lad?"

I shove my fingers through Pulse's eye sockets and drag

myself to my feet. Oberon bends to pick up the spear he's dropped, and I see that behind him, confusion explodes at the table on the bluff. Belial rolls slowly out from behind the cliff, and Raphael is running in my direction.

Oberon charges.

"Tell everything!" I yell, and I throw Pulse.

The pain of throwing him knocks me back to my knees.

Oberon swings the spear like a club over his head, trying to knock the skull out of the air as it whizzes past him. He misses, and Pulse goes tumbling mandible-over-occipital towards Mab and the Bearer of the Word.

"Oberon did it!" I hear Pulse wail. "The Avenue of Stones! Oberon put beans in the horse trough! Oberon was the mastermind!" He laughs as he yells, obviously highly amused.

I don't know if Mab can hear him, but Raphael, whose course has him running right towards Pulse, frowns, perplexed.

Oberon's not amused. He spins, grabbing at the grass and earth to keep himself upright, and then he goes galloping back towards the bluff.

The Legate rushes for the palanquin, his four golems bending at the knees to pick up their poles as he climbs in. Raphael streaks across the grass toward me. I'd love to show falcon and leave him in the dust, but I can't fly. But then Oberon dives for Pulse's skull and throws himself under Raphael's feet. They both go down in a tangle of green and flaming white.

I get up and run.

Eddie, Mike, and Adrian are at the Baobab. Eddie has his boomer out—it still looks like a spear—and is guarding the others. Adrian incants and wiggles his arms at the Baobab.

It isn't going to work. That tree is one of the oldest and most permanent things here. It preceded the Queendom, it's the tree on Mab's coat of arms, you can't just cast a little spell on it and expect it to open up for you.

Not that I have a better plan.

I run scattered, limping in irregular wheels and gasping from the pain. Belial oozes across the grass towards the tree, and Raphael is on his feet again, heading the same way. Mab shouts orders to the Rangers around her, and they take to the sky in bird forms, winging to close in on the Baobab.

The band is still disguised, but they've been identified.

At least we're within the Hedgerow. On fixed, permanent points, Mab's power is lessened.

I'm getting closer. I ought to reach them about the same time as the Legate, who is obviously working up some sort of spell himself—I can see the gestures and hear his chanting as his golems run. I'll get there in time to die with the others, I think.

That's hilarious.

Adrian shouts in frustration and turns away from the tree. Eddie begins unloading his boomer at the sky. *Boom!* Pump. *Boom!* Pump. *Boom!* Rangers show boy and girl and fall, stunned. Of course, the fall will hurt them more than the actual shots from the boomer, but Eddie's shots aren't useless.

Mike supports Adrian and pokes him with a finger, though the big guy looks over his shoulder at the tree. Behind the Baobab's root tails, each as thick around as his arm and many of them even thicker, Jim glowers. He pounds and kicks at the roots, but this has no effect. I could have told him to save his energy.

The Legate has out a candle like Adrian's, and he raises a lighter to its wick—

But Adrian's spell goes off first, and it's his good one. A blast of flame rockets towards the Legate and his palanquin. He throws himself out, tumbling heavy to the ground and dropping his candle and hat. The golems stop when he falls. They stand still, enduring the pounding flame in silence for several long seconds, and when it's over, they appear unfazed. A little singed, maybe.

The Legate scrambles aside to get out of the way of Adrian's firebolt. He steps on his own hat and moves away from the palanquin.

Why not? I see an opportunity. It's worth a try.

I shuffle over as the Legate moves away, preparing another spell, and I climb into the palanquin.

Ugh, I hurt. But the palanquin is soft, and it smells like

cardamom. It's surprisingly roomy, too, for one man. Two could lie on the cushions in here if they were friendly enough.

Adrian wavers but stays standing. He chants another spell.

And then Mike does something surprising. He's been looking over his shoulder at the Baobab every few seconds, and now he steps away from Adrian and takes something out of his pocket. I can't see what it is, it fits too well into his hand.

He pulls back his arm and throws.

I still can't see what the missile is, but it's small and colorful. Whatever the object is, it bounces off the knotted wood around one of the Baobab's mouths and falls to the ground. The tree's mouth twitches.

Belial and Raphael rush past me. Belial moves like a glacier in fast-forward, oozing across the ground. If he has a face, I can't tell where it is. Raphael runs with long, swooshing steps, arms floating out beside his body. Adrian hates the archangel. I'm not in love with him either.

Another firebolt. The Legate has raised some sort of arcane field, so it glances off the air around him, throwing up a wall of sparks. Belial slides sideways to get out of the way, though, and Raphael throws himself to the ground.

"Go!" I shout at the golems. It's a silly move, a reflex, but it works. They start moving forward at a quick jog. Into the fighting.

Mike throws something again. Again he hits the crusted outside of one of the tree's mouths.

Eddie pounds the roots of the Baobab with the butt of his boomer in between shots, but the blows accomplish nothing. Adrian slumps, but he's still standing. He looks exhausted. He raises his arms to cast a spell again, but nothing comes out. He weaves on his feet.

Raphael stands, laughing.

Mike throws a third time. And this time, he hits. Whatever it is he's thrown goes into the Baobab's mouth, which snaps shut.

And then nothing.

"That was pointless," I mutter. I can hear Pulse cackling

somewhere far behind me.

The Baobab shudders. Its bark wrinkles like a face showing distaste, and it bends over. It opens its mouth again to spit. Out comes a long string of brownish-red goo, and the Baobab doubles over.

I realize what Mike has thrown into the Baobab's mouth. It must have been one of his candy bars. And the Baobab is reacting the same way I reacted to my first Chocodile—with complete systemic rejection.

Mike hauls back and pitches another one, this time right into the Baobab's open maw.

The tree flexes in the middle, sharp and sudden, and spits the candy bar back out.

Mike hurls another one, and this time the Baobab tree lurches backward. Its roots all pull from the ground as it cringes under Mike's assault.

Jim runs out of his prison.

All the while, the golems continue to bear me into the fray, full tilt.

Raphael is talking, but I can't hear his words. He's probably trying to use his Whisper of Eden on the guys, but Jim isn't having any of it. He rips his sword from Eddie's jacket, cutting through the tough green fabric, and hurls himself at the angel.

I'm not sure how much damage Jim can really do, but he vaults off the back of a Queen's Ranger showing hippopotamus and slashes at Raphael's face. The angel staggers back.

Adrian fights to stay awake, and Belial is almost upon him.

"That way!" I yell to the golems. I point at Belial.

The golems are bigger than humans, and they have long legs under their kilts. We charge at Belial, and we do it fast.

Something else hurtles past us even faster.

The golems stagger to one side, and it takes me a moment to realize what I've seen. Beasts thunder from behind the palanquin and rush into the fray. There's a scuttling thing with enormous burrowing paws and mouths all over the back of its gigantic head. There's something like a praying mantis with a shark's head. There's Buzzard Betsy, and there are others.

The Wild Things are rampaging.

The palanquin crashes into Belial. The big, slimy ball of tentacles topples to the ground, clattering and roaring, and the foremost golems back up and immediately ram into him again. I have to grip the palanquin pole with my one good arm to avoid being tossed out. They've got enthusiasm, I'll give them that.

Belial shrieks and snaps in my direction. Something like a mouth opens amid all the tentacles. Long greenish teeth gleam dully and then snap together, slamming shut over the head of one of the golems.

With a shiver-inducing, spine-shattering squeal, Belial pulls back. His body undulates, sliding back and forth as it wobbles.

The golem's head is gone.

The golems back up two steps and charge again, ramming Belial's flank and tipping him over. The impact rattles me from my scalp to my toes. The headless golem runs just as fast and seems to hit just as hard as it did before.

I see Mab through the corner of my eye. She's riding on a white horse and charging into the center of things, her golden hair floating around her like a cloud of burning sunlight.

I look at the center myself and point the golems into the mass of arcing and flailing bodies. "Run!"

Jim fights Buzzard Betsy. He's picked up a spear from one of the Rangers, and now he swings his sword to keep Betsy at arm's length so he can poke her again and again with the spear.

Mike has Adrian slung over his back. The wizard is groggy, but I think he's conscious. For now. Mike curses, his face pale and sweating, and he fires his shooter into raging Wild Things. Eddie slams shells into his boomer.

Raphael hangs back, laughing and watching the monsters go to work. Mab rushes towards the Baobab, which has settled its roots again into the earth, and I have the horrible feeling that I know exactly what she's planning. As soon as she can get within earshot, she'll have the tree smash us to bits.

At least we're in a fixed point; that slows her down. Mab is most dangerous out in the fluid parts of the Queendom, where the Queendom shows whatever she wants it to.

Then Betsy takes a spear thrust into her body and Jim loses his grip on the weapon. He falls, and she rushes forward, trampling on the singer.

Boom! Eddie is at his side and firing. This will only piss Betsy off, I think, unless he can manage to hit her in the ankle or the eye.

The golems run forward, past Belial, past Raphael. The Legate sees me and shouts something, but in response, Mike fires his shooter at the man. The Legate ducks low to the ground, working up further spells.

Boom!

Grrrraaaaaaaack!

Betsy's cry is so loud and exultant, I look back at her again. She raises arms to the sky, howling and turning—

Her chain lies at her feet. Eddie has shot through the links, and the chain has fallen off.

Betsy roars and rushes. For a moment, I think she's running at me, and I brace myself to be overrun. But she pounds past me, shuffling at train-like speeds, and with extended claws, chases after her target.

The Legate.

He screams like a girl—*that's* funny—and runs.

And instantly, all the other chained monsters run amok. The Wild Things turn and savage each other with tusks. They bite into Belial the Tentacular and are bitten back. They trample the archangel Raphael under their feet.

Rangers scatter, throwing down their spears and cursing.

"Get on!" I yell to the band. Mike throws Adrian into the palanquin. The effort squeezes a sound out of him that might be a whimper, and then he jumps aboard, but Eddie Guitar and Jim Throat keep their feet. Eddie fires his boomer at Mab and her horse, forcing her to detour away from the Baobab.

That's good, but we still have to get out of here.

"That way!" I yell to the golems. Even the headless one hears me—I don't waste time wondering how—and they set off at a trot, slowed down only a little by the fact that they're now carrying many times more weight. To ease their burden a bit, I show falcon.

I bounce along in the palanquin, stunned and broken. Mike's bleeding through his tape, and his blood speckles my feathers red. I crane my bird head and see Mab rise before the Baobab, shouting words.

Surrounded by rampaging Wild Things, the Baobab slowly lifts its roots from the earth and turns to follow us.

At that moment, Eddie breaks away from the palanquin, splitting off to the right. "Eddie!" I cry, but he only hears a bird's call.

Jim joins him, and I see they're running for the musicians. Mab's band has stopped playing, and when they notice Jim and Eddie bearing down on them, they scatter. Jim grabs the thing that resembles a guitar, and Eddie, cursing, grabs the tambourines.

Oberon races at them, spear in hand, and Eddie shoots him. The boomer knocks Mab's consort to the grass.

I hear screaming behind me. I show girl to move my head and look around easier. The Baobab tree lifts half its roots from the ground, and the trunk splits with them. I see reddish wood in the underside of the tree, and then the monstrous thing lurches in our direction. It must cover two hundred feet in a single step.

I've seen the Baobab a million times, and I've always known it could move, but I've never seen it do so before now. And it's staggering. It's like watching living geography, like seeing an entire landscape pick itself up and run.

WHAM!

The ground shakes as the Baobab slams into it. Earth and grass rise and fall in a literal wave from the shock, knocking Jim and Eddie both off their feet. Jim rolls, but Eddie loses the tambourines and scrambles to recover them.

WHAM!

Another giant step.

"Adrian!" I poke the wizard. "Do something!"

He stirs himself slightly, breathing deep.

"*Chingón!*" Mike curses at him. The big guy grabs Adrian by the hair and drags him upright, pointing behind us with the barrel of his shooter. "Big tree!" he snaps, face quivering. "You gotta help us!"

Adrian shakes himself like a dog coming out of water. He gropes around his person and finds the Eye and his candle stub. Poor boy. But if anyone can help us at this moment, it's Adrian.

WHAM!

Dirt clods rain down on the palanquin's canopy. Jim and Eddie fall to the ground again. The golems are amazingly surefooted, which is a good thing. The earth rises and falls under their feet, and they keep running.

I can see the opening in the Hedgerow ahead. It's a simple gap, thirty feet across. Behind it, I can see the nearest of the Stones jutting out of the mist that always shrouds the Avenue.

A dozen Rangers crowd in it, spears braced against the ground and firmly pointed at us.

"That was too close!" I yell.

Mike looks ahead of us and fires his shooter. *Bang! Bang! Bang!* He manages to knock down one of the Rangers, but it won't be enough. They don't have to stop us, not really. All they have to do is slow us down for a moment or two, and the Baobab will stomp us flat.

Or maybe it will imprison us in its roots again, and we'll be at the mercy of the Legate and Belial and Mab.

"*Caray*, do something!"

Adrian wipes sweat off his forehead. He doesn't look good, he's pale and blinking.

"You can do this." I show him cute girl.

The Baobab's root-foot reaches the apex of its step, and I peer up at it. Roots dangle down like tentacles, writhing and poking at the air.

"*Per Volcanum ignem mitto!*" Adrian shouts.

The firebolt rips away the palanquin's canopy; Adrian is shooting up. I watch the bolt lance into the writhing nest of the Baobab's roots and splash like red-hot glowing liquid all along the underside.

Adrian collapses forward onto one hand. He's holding

himself propped upright, but his breathing still sounds suspiciously like snores.

"I hope that hurts!" Mike hollers.

The Baobab totters on one foot, knocked off balance.

Behind us, a cadre of Rangers coalesces around Mab. Mab rides on our tail, spear in hand, and the Rangers follow behind her. With them comes Belial. Buzzard Betsy is still chasing the Legate around the field.

"What about in front of us?" I yell.

Mike swivels and fires his shooter at the Rangers in the gap again. Eddie, running at our side and slightly behind us with Jim, joins in with his boomer. They have no effect. The Rangers wait for us with flirtatiously bared teeth and sharp spears.

The Baobab totters overhead—

CRACK!

Something shatters, and I don't immediately know what it is.

Guns go off close to me, filling my vision with white flashes, but the Rangers hold their ground. Mab closes the gap behind.

"Jump!" I scream at the golems.

They jump.

An explosive shattering sound behind me turns my head as we sail through the air. I see a cloud of splinters snapping from the roots of the Baobab still in the ground, and I realize it's shattered its own footing and lost its balance. The Baobab begins to fall forward.

We sail over the heads of the Rangers in the gap, spears poking at the legs and feet of the vaulting golems.

Ahead of us, gray mists swirl, and several of the Avenue's Stones come into view. I look behind, and I can see the fury on Mab's face, framed in gold. The Rangers in the gap turn to stab at us as we fly over, and Jim and Eddie bowl into them from behind.

Rangers scatter in all directions, showing vole, spider, sloth, girl, boy, and ocelot. Jim and Eddie burst through and onto the Avenue. The golems land, light on their feet despite their bulk, and keep running.

CRASH!!

Behind us, the Baobab smashes to the ground, its long, arboreal body lying right through the middle of the gap.

Chapter Nine

The golems rattle up the Avenue of Stones.

The Avenue can be infinite if you let it. It only has two ends, but what lies at each of those two ends is entirely up to the traveler, within a range of choices. The Avenue doesn't go anywhere you could want to go in the Queendom, but it does go to the Baobab, the Palace, and the Crossroads, as well as a few other old, old places. The fixed places.

"The Push!" I shout to Adrian.

He nods sluggishly and sets to work on a spell, looking at me through the Eye and muttering. As he prepares, though the golems run at full speed, the ground shoots past beneath our feet and the Stones whiz by, the gap in the Hedgerow behind us doesn't get any further away. The Baobab thrashes, trying to get up, but it may need help—I've never heard of the Baobab falling over before, and I have a hard time seeing how it can stand. Still, it tries, bending in the middle and pushing off the ground.

"Come on," Eddie mutters. Jim runs, looking over his shoulder, pseudo-guitar in one hand and sword in the other.

Rangers begin to bound over the trunk of the Baobab. The fliers show winged forms and zip over the tree, bombarding the ground as boys and girls with spears. Others race beneath the arcing trunk on four legs, and some clamber over the top with hands and feet.

Boom! Bang! Bang!

Mike and Eddie open fire. At least we aren't in an enclosed space here, so I don't feel like my hearing is immediately and permanently damaged. Still, it's loud. I grab my other fighting stick and get ready to throw it. A magpie and a kingfisher bullet down in my direction, beaks snapping angrily.

"*Per Mercurium manum distraho*," Adrian finally says, and the Push slides off me.

"Go!" I yell at the golems, but they don't need it. They're already running, and as the Push comes off us, we burst forward. I will us to the Crossroads.

Not before Squirt Kingfisher and Slouch Magpie hit the back of the palanquin, though. Slouch hits showing girl and stabbing with a spear, and Squirt shows monkey. He immediately jumps onto the face of the nearest golem.

I knock the first spear thrust aside with my stick. If I weren't beaten and crippled, I'd grab the spear with my other hand and throw Slouch off the ride. Instead I roll, pinning the spear under my body.

The move traps my arm under my own chest, leaving my head exposed, and Slouch takes advantage. She shows lobster, and big red claws clamp down on both my ears.

I scream.

Something heavy falls on top of me, squishing all the breath from my lungs. My ears feel tugged and torn—

Bang!

And then Slouch Magpie is gone.

Mike rolls off me. I'm even bloodier than before.

"Sorry," he says. "I didn't want to shoot you in the head by accident."

I'm afraid if I reward him by showing him pretty girl I might distract him. So I just smile, nod, and pat his arm.

I hear monkey howling and look back. Squirt Kingfisher has torn and bitten big chunks out of the golem's face, but it continues running, indifferent. Squirt roars his frustration and jumps again, not in my direction but at Jim.

Jim stops just for a moment and swings the guitar, holding it by the neck. Its body is heavy wood, and it slams hard into Squirt's face. With a loud *twang*, the instrument shatters. Squirt shows kingfisher and flaps in midair, dazed, which just gives Jim time to swing the neck back again from the other direction. He cracks Squirt square in the middle with a meaty thump, and the Ranger sails off into the mist.

Jim tosses aside the mangled instrument and runs again. He's behind us now, and Eddie is off to the side. Behind Jim come Rangers, and I can hear terrible shrieking and roaring sounds in the mist. Wild Things.

I continue to will us in the direction of the Crossroads. I can feel the unseen fingers of the Push sliding off my body as Adrian's interference continues to help. "Well done, Adrian," I tell him. He murmurs back to me groggily, no real words.

"Dammit," Eddie snaps. "Back to the tambourines again. I just can't get away from these things."

Mike struggles to situate himself on the bouncing palanquin. The conveyance was really built for one man in comfort, and the three of us are squashed too close. I show falcon, which helps, but Mike still has to be careful to avoid sitting on Adrian, who struggles to remain conscious. "Yeah, why the instruments, anyway?" Mike asks.

Eddie shakes his head. "Just a hunch," he says. "A terrible, terrible hunch."

"Get up, Adrian," Mike says. He prods the wizard and shakes him.

An earsplitting roar shatters the mist behind us. Dark shadows move behind the shrouding mist. They're too far away and too obscured to see any details, but the shadows are so wide and so tall that it's hard to imagine they belong to anything but the Baobab.

"Ah, hell." Eddie sees it too.

"How long until we get there?" Mike asks.

I huddle up into a corner of the palanquin and show girl. "We're almost there now," I tell him. The mist is thicker now. I can't see our pursuit anymore, though I can hear the animal cries of Rangers and the great, thudding footsteps of the Baobab. I can feel the Push on my body, reasserting itself. Adrian must be losing his battle to stay awake.

ROAAAAAAAARRRR!!!

That's a cry I've heard before.

"Rahab?" Mike asks.

"Rahab," I agree. "Herself. The great old dragon. Guardian of the Crossroads."

At that moment I also hear a loud buzzing sound.

"Maybe she won't see us," Mike suggests. "We can sneak past her."

"She'll see," I tell him. "Rahab has very good eyesight. If the mist works to anyone's advantage, it's hers."

"We have to go faster," Eddie says. He's panting with effort, so I don't know how he imagines that we possibly can. "We need to try to run past this thing as fast as we can before it can harm us. And get Adrian up."

Getting Adrian up is an excellent idea. The Push is painful, and I'm not sure if it's because his spell has failed or because something is strengthening the mechanism of my banishment. Either way, I want out.

The first Zavuv bounces off the palanquin's canopy and disappears into the mist, but the second dive-bombs Mike, sinking its mandibles into the leather of his jacket before he can get his shooter around and pointed at it. *Bang!* That fly, too, disappears, leaving behind it a faint, rotting stink that is made worse by the moisture in the air.

I stroke Adrian's brow and show him attractive girl. "Time to wake up, big boy," I murmur to him. He stirs. He's not asleep, but he's close.

Jim puts on a burst of speed and catches up. I duck, thinking he's going to charge right through the palanquin, but at the last second he jumps instead and lands on the back of a golem, riding it piggyback.

The golem doesn't bat an eye. It just groans a bit and keeps running, Jim's long black hair flapping out into the mist behind them.

Eddie is flagging, but he manages to follow Jim's example. He has to hold on with his elbows because one hand is occupied with his boomer and the other holds two tambourines. The instruments rattle noisily on the golem's chest as it runs.

"Faster!" I yell to the golems, and they speed up. The foremost runners plow through Zvuvim, shattering them into scraps of dusty-smelling black fiber. The chattering and buzzing noise becomes intense around us, but the golems don't slow down.

"Man." Adrian shakes his head and looks around at the palanquin bearers. "I gotta get me some of these things."

As he speaks, the Push lessens. He's reasserting his magic. Or maybe it just cheers me up to see him awake again.

Mike has a spear. I'm not sure where he got it—maybe it's the one Slouch Magpie was attacking me with—and he bats at the incoming Zvuvim with it. The Rangers disappear behind us into the mist, and the ground rises sharply beneath the golems' feet.

"This is it!" I snap. "The Eye, Adrian!"

Adrian looks through the Eye, and his body immediately stiffens in fright. "Son of a bitch!" he squeals. "Left!"

The golems obey him instantly, swerving off the Avenue of Stones and running across the hill laterally. The air-clotting swarm of giant flies around us immediately lessens.

A blast of light and heat hits the road we've just left behind. It isn't fire because it's white and smells like ozone. It's more like a bolt of electricity, like lightning has just struck the Avenue behind us. It smells of burnt flesh, and worse.

I hear the yelp of a dog and a soft sobbing sound.

ROAAAAAAAARRRRR!

"Rahab," I mutter to no one in particular.

Our path across the hill is taking us to the summit, behind one of the Stones that stand in a ring around the Crossroads.

"Adrian!" I slap the wizard. "Can you see the Crossroads?"

"I dunno about the Crossroads," Eddie shouts, "but I can see *that!*"

I look back to see what he's talking about. I'm jostled by the running golems, but another bolt of lightning shatters the sky, cutting the mist apart and blowing a crater in the packed earth of the Avenue. In its momentary blaze and the shining eye-echoes that follow, I see a huge, armless figure stalking up the hill to the Crossroads.

WHAM!

The Baobab's root-foot slams into the slope, and it draws itself up. About its flanks swarm flapping shapes that might be Queen's Rangers, fighting for space with the cloud of Zvuvim. At its feet run strange, undulating Wild Things, the baby-esca beast, worms, Buzzard Betsy, and worse. I see them for a moment, and then the flash is gone and they disappear again.

"Forget that!" Mike shouts. "The road—where's the road? Where do we go?"

The golems rush between two Stones twenty feet apart, and into the Crossroads.

"Stop!" I cry, and they do, like a machine.

Immediately in front of us, a clawed foot digs into the earth. Its talons are easily as long as my body, and as the beast steadies its balance by gripping, those talons dig furrows as large and as deep as graves. The leg sprouting out of the top of the foot rises into the mist and disappears. The leg is shackled, and I see the first few links before they're swallowed in the mist. Each is the size of an automobile, huge and black and clanking.

"*Huevos,*" Mike breathes.

Adrian claps the Eye to his face and looks around.

"Roads …" he mutters. "There are tons of 'em. Roads in every direction. Roads going everywhere. This is the crossroads to beat all crossroads."

All I see is mist.

"Great," Eddie barks. "Find the one we need!"

The buzzing gets louder, and flies start to swarm around us again. Mike batters them away from the palanquin with his borrowed spear, and Jim and Eddie dismount.

"Quiet!" I hiss at them.

"Sooner rather than later!" Eddie adds. He shoves both tambourines around one forearm and swings his boomer like a club, knocking flies out of the air with its butt. The boomer *thuds* wetly into the Zvuvim, the tambourines adding a pleasing jangle to the blow.

"Water, water, everywhere," Adrian mutters. "You know."

Mike scrambles off the palanquin and attacks with his spear. He winces with each blow, but he kills flies. I hear hooting and roaring of beasts from the Avenue of Stones, and I want to help. I roll over and drop off the palanquin, wincing at the pain in my ribs, head, and arms as I hit the ground.

I'm unarmed. I can't usefully show a good fighting shape. What do I have to contribute?

The golems stand, impassive. I remember them fighting on the rooftop of the meatpacking plant in Kansas. "Attack!" I call to them. Nothing. I point to the cloud of giant flies and say it again. "Attack the Zvuvim!" Rahab's much bigger and scarier, but she doesn't appear to have noticed us yet.

The golems groan. The headless one takes one hand away from its bearer pole to pat itself around the stump of its neck. None of them attack.

I guess they're showing palanquin bearers right now, not fighting golems. Or something. I have no idea how golems work.

The buzzing of flies grows more intense. Humanoid shapes rumble towards us out of the mist, preceded by a shrill bellow.

Graaaaraaargh!

"Where there are Zvuvim, there's a Baal," I say to Adrian. "There's one for your collection."

"Too long."

"Twitch!" Eddie snaps, and he presses his shooter into my hand. "Use this!"

Then he raises his boomer to his shoulder and fires into the onward-shambling Baalim. Mike joins him, and Jim protects them both from the flies, slashing with his sword and ducking in and around the palanquin for cover. Zvuvim swarm over all four of the golems, biting and gouging. For all the reaction the golems show, the flies might as well not be there.

"I don't know how to use it!" I protest. It's something of an exaggeration. I've seen lots of TV shows in late-night motel rooms in recent months, not to mention the shooting I've seen in person from the other guys.

"Point and squeeze!" Eddie barks. "It doesn't have a safety; just point and squeeze!"

"That's good," I say, the earth under my feet shuddering. "The last thing I'd want now is safety."

"Over there!" Adrian points directly beyond the Baalim, past Rahab's earth-gouging claw.

I forget about the shooter for a moment. "You sure?"

He winks at me through the Eye. "I'm sure."

Rahab shifts, and it's like the earth spins. Her claw scrapes back as she adjusts her stance, battering both the Baalim. One flies back into the mist and disappears, and the other staggers sideways between two Stones and out of sight, squealing like a murdered pig.

Rahab's face looms large over us. It's the size of a bus. Fangs like spears gnash against each other, and slobber hits the earth, carving smoking pits with each gallon-sized drop. She's gold and blue and green, colored vaguely like the sea. Her chain rattles as she moves, a dark noise as loud as thunder.

"Gotta get me one of these, too," Adrian quips. He doesn't mean it. I can hear in his voice that he's fighting off sleep just at the sight of Rahab. That's not good.

Boom! Boom! Boom!

Eddie fires at the side of Rahab's muzzle. His shots do nothing but raise sparks as they glance off her scales. I've seen one of Rahab's discarded scales; it was larger than a dinner plate, twice as thick, and hard as steel. No surprise that the shots don't do anything, but I point the shooter at her and squeeze anyway.

I hit her right in the snout with the first shot, but I'm not expecting the force with which the weapon jumps in my hand or how quickly it shoots. After the first shot, a stream of projectiles goes high, glancing up Rahab's neck and then disappearing into the mist.

"Son of a bitch," Adrian mutters.

Rahab's jaws gape, but she hesitates. Adrian looks at her, and specifically at her eye.

He's seen it—the tiny, silvery flaw on the surface of her eye where, ages ago, her conqueror smashed out a little piece of Rahab.

And she's seen what Adrian's holding in his hand—a silvery fragment like a bit of polished glass.

Adrian looks through the Eye at Rahab the dragon, the source of much of his power. He sags.

Rahab raises her head and bellows. Lightning sizzles from her muzzle, blasting Zvuvim to nothing and scorching Stones black. She rears onto her hind legs, and her front claws jump into the air above us. I empty the shooter out into her belly, but I know it's a waste of time.

Eddie pushes Mike and me. He's cursing, trying to get us to move, but I can't hear his words. All I can think about is how enormous Rahab is and how powerful and beautiful she looks. And she's about to destroy us because the Crossroads is her place and we're not welcome here, and because little Adrian Pew has been carrying a piece of her around for years, and she wants it back.

CRASH!

Something plows into Rahab from behind. In the mist, I can't make it out, but it's so vast it must be the Baobab. Rahab falls sideways with the shadow pressing on top of her, lurching away into the mist, too big to disappear entirely.

But Rahab's movement has opened up the entrance to the Avenue. Gibbering shrieks and bloodcurdling howls bounce along the earth in our direction.

"Go!" I yell at Adrian. He snaps out of his reverie and scuttles across the Crossroads towards the path he's indicated. Mike and Eddie follow, and Jim grabs my arm.

He looks at me, quizzical.

"I'm right behind you," I say. He hesitates a moment, nods, then runs after the others.

I limp over to the palanquin and tumble into it. I see the Wild Things come out of mist. Buzzard Betsy is one of them, once again chained around her waist. There are wolves with multiple heads, too, and vast mouths without apparent bodies and snakes and insects and cats with no eyes, and if they catch me, I'm dead for sure.

"Run!" I yell to the golems, and I point at the Wild Things.

They sprint, and I immediately roll out of the palanquin.

"Mab's shiny belly, please let this work," I mutter as I fall. I have a vision of myself getting trampled flat by golem feet, so I cover the back of my neck with my hand to protect it and try to huddle into a ball.

The impact hurts, and I groan.

But the golems crash past me without pounding me, and without stopping.

I throw myself onto my feet and run. I spare just a glance for the Wild Things. They're confused by the palanquin, which is hilarious, and they all react differently. Some run. Some scamper out of the way. Betsy grabs a leading golem and tries to rip him to pieces. She manages to tear off one huge muscular arm with jaws, but the other clings tightly to the palanquin pole.

I keep running.

ROOOAAAARRR!

Rahab hurls the Baobab off her body and away from her. I hear a mighty and terrible *CRAAAACCK* as Stones tip over and shatter and the Baobab's vast, shadowy bulk disappears into the mist.

Lightning crashes, and I think it must be Rahab striking again. I smell scorched Wild Thing, but I don't slow down. Rahab's tail switches out of my way, clearing my path for the exit. I see a long, dark passage between two Stones. Eddie crouches at the edge of one of the Stones, taking cover behind it and firing his boomer at a Baal Zavuv, which has recovered from being thrown around by Rahab and looms up to threaten my companions.

Jim cuts down flies. Mike shoots them.

Adrian stands in front of them all, beckoning and calling to me. He holds the Eye in his hand, and he looks through it at me and at the dragon around whose feet I lurch.

"Come on, Twitch!" he yells. "Last one in is a—"

CRASHHHHHH!

A bolt of lightning slams down into the place where Adrian is standing.

Suddenly, he's gone.

CHAPTER TEN

I fall down. I hit the ground hard, pain jolting through my body and streaks of light flashing beneath my eyelids. I struggle forward on both knees and one shoulder for a few moments before I can again lurch to my feet.

Adrian's still gone.

I stagger forward. This isn't funny, but beyond that, I'm astonished at how much it hurts me. Adrian can't be gone. But if he's gone, he's gone, just another dead human, that's how they all go, and I shouldn't think twice about it.

Only there are tears running down my cheeks.

"No!" I yell, and I rush forward to where he stood.

There's a crater. And lying in the bottom of the crater, the Eye, in a pile of greasy ash. Greasy ash that used to be Adrian.

"No!" I yell again. I'm off balance, my mind isn't working. I should be running down the road with the rest of the band, headed to our planned rendezvous with the Infernal Princes. Eddie is yelling at me, waving at me to come running to him, but I can't. My ears ring. I'm deaf, I'm yelling, I don't know what words are coming out of my mouth or even what exactly I'm showing at the moment.

I bend down and pick up the Eye. It's hard to do, my muscles hurt so much.

As I straighten and look up, I see Rahab above me. She's enormous, far bigger than any moving thing has a right to be. I hold up the Eye and shake it at her.

"See this?" I yell. "I'm keeping it!"

ROAAAAARRR!

She shakes her body, and her chains clank like school buses being chewed into shards. Coming around her flanks from behind her are onrushing Wild Things and Queen's Rangers. I should care, but I don't. Not enough.

"It was my friend's!" I shout. Which is crazy, because it was Rahab's first, and Rahab obviously knows it.

She rears back. The motion is like the movement of a mountain, a ripple of steely, scale-encased muscles back from enormous claws through haunches and flanks, the thrash of a tail that sends two of the Stones flying into mists and perdition. She's so tall, her head ought to disappear into the fog as she rises, but white electric fire crackles in her open mouth and eyes, and that fire cuts through the mist and keeps her visible.

"And now it's mine!" I shake it.

Rahab plunges forward. I'm going to die.

Clink.

A metallic jangle. Not Rahab's chains, but something much softer and yet more piercing. Rahab's chains rattle with the sound of darkness, but this is a lighter tone. One, and then another, and then a third, and then a rhythm springs into being that seems to bear with it a melody of gold and wind.

Eddie is playing the two tambourines. The tambourine—the timbrel—is an instrument so old it predates the throwing down of the dragon, the laying of the Crossroads, and the building of the Outer Bounds. It may be the first instrument, maybe as old as Herself is.

And Eddie's really, really good with the tambourine.

Rahab freezes. She hangs over me, nostrils big enough to crawl inside dilating over and over, exhaling a warm, wet miasma into my lungs. I stand beneath her fangs, and they're taller than I am. Her claw, suspended in midair over my head, is big enough to slice me open from crown to heel without slowing down.

But she waits.
Then Eddie starts to sing.

> *I will sing unto the Lord, for he hath triumphed gloriously:*
> *The horse and his rider hath he thrown into the sea.*
> *The Lord is my strength and song, and he is become my*
> *salvation:*
> *He is my God, and I will prepare him an habitation;*
> *My father's God, and I will exalt him.*
> *The Lord is a man of war:*
> *The Lord is his name.*

I don't recognize the words, but they sound like Bible. Well, Bible language makes for terrible music, apparently. It doesn't rhyme, and it doesn't scan. It has no bounce or swing. Eddie is merely chanting. Still, somehow, the tambourines provide both rhythm and melody, turning his words into a song.

The dragon swivels her head and glares at Eddie Guitar.

I want to defy Rahab, but I can't. I want to attack her, but that's insane. All I am now is two legs that more or less work and one wounded arm. The rest of me is out of commission, and I've thrown away both my fighting sticks.

I shuffle across the toasted, furrowed earth, conscious of the vast girth of the primordial reptile beside and above me. All she has to do is shudder, and her bulk will squash me flat as a leaf.

But she doesn't shudder. She stares at Eddie, who keeps singing.

> *Thy right hand, O Lord, is become glorious in power:*
> *Thy right hand, O Lord, hath dashed in pieces the enemy.*
> *And in the greatness of thine excellency*
> *Thou hast overthrown them that rose up against thee:*
> *Thou sentest forth thy wrath, which consumed them as*
> *stubble.*

"What are you doing?" I ask Eddie as I reach him, but he ignores me and concentrates on his playing and on his words.

He holds his head at an unnatural angle, looking steeply up, his eye fixed and glittering.

I follow his gaze, and see that he's staring into Rahab's eye. "Get moving," he grunts to me out of the corner of his mouth. He doesn't miss a beat in the elaborate weave-and-rattle of his two hands. "They're almost on us."

A deep baying like the noise of hounds reminds me of the Wild Things. I turn and see Buzzard Betsy in the fore, shambling at high speed around Rahab's haunch. With her are the ugly thing with the baby-like appendage for a lure, a pack of headless, six-legged hounds with ragged mouths in their chests, and a snake with a human face.

Rahab snorts.

Eddie sings again. I shuffle past him as quickly as I can. I'm tempted to look through the Eye at what's happening, but something about that idea feels wrong in my own mind. Premature. Inappropriate. I curl my fist around the lens, imagining the wrath in old Rahab's heart at the sight of me.

And with the blast of thy nostrils the waters were gathered together,
The floods stood upright as an heap,
And the depths were congealed in the heart of the sea

When Eddie finishes his song, he snaps both his tambourines rapidly several times in the direction of the Wild Things.

"Attack!" he barks.

It's his I'm-the-boss voice, the tone that gets Mike away from the bar and onto the stage and sometimes even wakes Adrian up ... *woke* Adrian up ... but it can't possibly work on Rahab the dragon. I limp faster and prepare to be squashed.

ROAAARRR!

Rahab whips around, and for a moment I think I am about to die. Her tail hurtles towards me through the air like an earthquake in corporeal form. Eddie and I both drop to the dirt, and I expect that the monster's next move will be to whip that same tail vertically into the sky and then slam it down on top of us, reducing us to paste—

But Rahab lunges forward, away from us.

She spits lightning, the crackling, white fire of it blasting a deep hole in the unruly mass of beasts rushing our way. The headless hounds are vaporized. Queen's Rangers and Zvuvim swarming among the beasts shriek as they are crushed or hurl themselves out of the way. Rahab smashes one of her forelegs down—*SPLAT!*—and the human-faced snake splits into two flailing halves.

Buzzard Betsy escapes their fate. Mockers shriek about her in a cloud, *hyoo-hyoo-hyoo-waaaaoooo!* She charges right over the crater where Adrian died. The mist swirls around and behind her like a cloak, and she lifts her talons high—

Eddie raises his boomer—

And Rahab's tail sweeps over our heads again. Big and strong as a train, the enormous whip of scale and muscle plows into Betsy. The monstrous queen, eater of children and once-custodian of my fellow prankster Pulse Lemur, *ooomphs* uncomfortably and achieves sudden liftoff.

Gracefully as any bird, with hair, dress, and limbs trailing behind her like the dust of a comet, she launches into the sky and is gone.

"Stop staring and run!"

Eddie jerks me by the elbow and drags me with him.

I can't run, but I hobble as fast as I can.

Zvuvim clack and buzz more intensely behind me. Those things only have any brains around the Baalim, I know, so at least one of the big, pig-faced lads must have recovered himself. Ahead of me, Mike's shooter flares in the mist, and Eddie's boomer barks beside me. I don't know what they're even aiming at; as we move away from Rahab, the mist thickens again, and I can't see a thing.

I hear hoofbeats behind me. I try, but I can't run any faster.

The air changes. A dark, warm blast hits me in the face. It sweeps mist away, ripping it into tatters, and I see that the Stones have changed too. They aren't the squat, thick menhirs of the Avenue and the Crossroads anymore. They're fangs, jutting up and curving inward over my head to sharp points. Dark lichen scabs them over, and a dim reddish light makes the lichen look like fresh black blood.

Sunset. The light is red because the sun is setting.

I've never been down this road. I'm just following Jim's lead, and Adrian's. I know where it's taking us, though—this was once the City of Ainok. Mud sucks at my ankles, and the track ahead of me winds down among jagged, spiky rocks to a stagnant sea and the gaping mouth of a cavern. Crumbling ruins, gigantic, moldering walls and columns, jut from the rotting sea and stand tall and lonely at the top of the hill above me. This was once a place of unspeakable beauty.

Giant flies buzz around us, and Eddie swats them away.

"Stop, Pony!"

The command is in Oberon's anxious whistle of a voice, and I ignore it, staggering faster. Eddie still drags me by the elbow. He shoots a glance over my head and keeps going.

"Stop!"

This voice is Mab's. Out of sheer reflex, the habit of thousands of years, my legs stop working and I almost topple forward into the mud.

Eddie turns with me to look. Oberon stands up to his ankles in mud, his bottle-green uniform spattered black. He holds a spear in both hands, and behind him, Mab sits astride a big black horse. The horse is one of her Rangers, of course, Duck Percheron, but he isn't going to show anything but big strong horse as long as the Queen's on his shoulders. The other Rangers haven't emerged from the mist swirling behind the royal couple. Maybe they're fighting Rahab and all the monsters. Mab's hands are empty, but she has something at her side that might be a spear.

And she's showing powerful, seductive Mab. And Eddie has noticed. His nostrils are flared wide, and his teeth are gritted.

"Eddie," I say, and I squeeze his hand. He doesn't squeeze mine back, but he does raise his boomer. It's a tentative gesture, only half-convinced.

I hear shooting and Spanish curses. Behind me, lower down along the muddy road, Mike struggles against the big flies.

"Surely," Mab says to Eddie Guitar, and she slowly blinks twice to tell him that she really means it. She's turned on the charm so thick that it almost overwhelms *me*, and I'm not even the target. "This wretched creature is of no interest to you."

She gestures at me. I'm the wretched creature, and it hits me in that moment that the Queendom is not my home. It hasn't been for a long, long time. I feel like a wretched creature right now, broken and run over and discarded. Still, I'm not dead yet.

I pull at Eddie's hand. "Come on, Eddie," I say gently.

He shakes his head and sucks in a deep breath. I'm not sure he's heard me.

Oberon takes a step closer. Duck Percheron snorts and raises a hoof in open threat. I wish I had something to fight with. If I weren't so beat up, I'd show pony and kick Mab's consort into jelly. I spit at Oberon, and he hesitates.

"Leave the caitiff," Mab urges Eddie. Her smile is rich, like an overgrown forest. "Bring the half-devil back with me, to the Queendom."

Caitiff, that's me. She's right. I'm not one of hers anymore. And this whole plan of mine to get Azazel to forgive me was misbegotten from the start. It was never Azazel who was angry with me. It was Mab herself, and maybe Belial. And nothing I've done in crossing the Queendom will endear me to either of them.

I could grab the hoof, maybe, and hand it over. But Adrian's dead and Mab hates me and the only family I have left are this nameless rock-and-roll band, so I'm not going to betray them to her.

Where is Jim anyway? I look around behind me and see why he and Mike are delayed. One of the Baalim is on the road, and Jim fights it hand to hand with his sword. Mike tries to cover his back against Zvuvim attacks, but there are a lot of them and he has only the one shooter.

I show pretty girl to Eddie, as pretty as I can. "Let's go, big fella," I say to him. It feels like a betrayal, but I can't figure out who the victim is—Adrian? Eddie? I pull on his hand and try to lead him back, away from Mab.

Oberon steps forward to fill the space, the pointy end of his spear held in my direction.

"You don't need Jacob bar Azazel," Mab says in a throaty voice. She's showing the most alluring Mab I've ever seen. "Everything you need is in the Queendom."

She raises her arm, and I'm stunned to see what she holds in her hand.

It's Azazel's hoof.

The thing we chased across the desert for, our ticket for negotiating with His Lowness. I'd assumed Jim still had it. He's been carrying it around taped to his belly since we got it. Of course, once they captured Jim, it must have been easy to take it from him.

But if Mab has the hoof, what is she after? And the Legate and Raphael and Belial—why did they hold Jim in the Baobab's roots, and why are they chasing us now?

Do they want Jim himself?

"Everything you need is with us," I say to Eddie. I'm confused and I'm desperate. I might be lying. I'm showing as pretty a girl as I know how, but I'm nothing next to Mab's glory.

Eddie scowls and yanks his hand away.

"Eddie …" Mab smiles.

Eddie's eyes are glazed with madness. He points his boomer at Duck Percheron's forehead, and the big black horse shies back half a step.

"Everything I need," Eddie grinds out slowly, "is at *home*."

Mab's eyes flash fire. She opens her mouth—

Boom!

Eddie hits Duck right between the eyes. The boomer slugs won't kill him, but they won't feel pleasant, either. Duck falls backward, and in confusion and pain, he shows a fat brown quail.

Mab collapses on top of him. They hit the ground together, just as the Ranger flashes from quail to chubby boy. I think he's in an intermittent, unstable showing when his Queen squashes his head, forcing a sound out of his lungs that is part squeaky chirp and part strangled grunt.

Oberon spins around and gasps.

Eddie lunges forward, snatches the hoof from Mab's grasp. Oberon raises his spear over his shoulder to hurl it at Eddie.

I show pony. Only for a moment, because my ribs hurt and this showing is heavy. I show pony just long enough to bite Oberon on the back of his neck.

Hard.

"Ponyyyyyyy!" my former friend howls. His spear cast misses, and he tumbles into the mud.

I show girl and run. Stagger, anyway.

Eddie doesn't need any persuading to follow. He pumps out three quick shots with his boomer and then he's with me, sloshing through the mud, boomer swinging in one hand and the other clutching Azazel's hoof to his chest.

Just as we catch up to him, Jim disposes of the Baal Zavuv. He does it like a parody of a matador, standing in front of one of the stone fangs until the last moment of the Baal's head-first charge and then dropping flat to the mud. The Baal crashes into the stone and bursts both its own eyes, spattering black goo crawling with larval flies over the lichen, the stone, and Jim.

Jim stands and runs his long sword through the demon's head, putting an abrupt end to its frantic shudders.

"You forgot something!" Eddie barks to Jim. He waves the hoof.

Jim nods, but Eddie doesn't offer him the hoof fragment, and Jim doesn't ask for it.

The pain is so sharp I can barely see. I find myself leaning on Jim as we run. Flies buzz around us, but they're brainless and do us no harm. Behind us come things, an army, or maybe a wall of beasts. I don't look, I just hear the gigantic thumping of thousands of feet and hooves in the mud.

The orange-red light gives way to dark blue, and we drop down to the edge of the sea. I see a single star, brighter than any star has a right to be, above the open maw of the cavern on the seashore. The sea itself is sucking mud, strewn with the swaying carcasses of animals. Half-submerged skulls stare at me in accusation, fleshless limbs point.

We run, clattering over a beach of bones. Eyeless birds cry and swoop without aim. The mud feels like it has fingers concealed within it, trying to drag me down. I hold tight to the Eye. I don't know what to do with it. I don't know if we're going to make it. I don't have anything left to fight with.

The great sloping brow of the cavern shuts out most of the twinkling stars. Out of the mud, we rise haggardly on stone steps worn deeply in the center. We're covered in filth, and we stink of death. Every step Jim takes bounces my head on his shoulder, and at the top of the steps, he sets me gently down.

Gently, but I gasp in pain.

And fear.

"You!" I hiss.

At the top of the stairs is a double door. The doors are enormous slabs of cold iron, maybe thirty feet tall and twenty feet wide together. I tremble at the thought of how much that iron door would hurt if it fell on me. Knockers wrought of similar iron, each five feet across, hang fifteen feet off the ground; each knocker is shaped like a skeletal human ouroboros, twisted in a ring of pain to seize itself by the ankles. The skulls' mouths are open as if to scream.

Standing in front of the door, holding the reins of her meat-eating horse in one hand and an old black shooter in the other, is the Marked Woman. Her face tattoos swirl at me menacingly, as they did when she burned and tortured me in the restroom in Kansas.

She smiles, and I can't read it. "You guys get around."

Jim snaps mud from his arms and chest and snorts. "Twitch," he says to me, and points up at the knockers, "this is the sort of thing I'd ask you to handle. Ordinarily."

"Ordinarily," I say, "I'd be happy to handle it. But I've had a bad day, and I can't really fly right now." Quite apart from the fact that the doors and knockers are made of unforged iron.

"I can," the Marked Woman says, and she steps like she's going to remount her horse.

"I got it," says Eddie. He pumps his boomer once and shoots the doors.

The doors ring with a deep *GONG!* The sound hangs in the air like snow. I turn to look at the road behind us.

Mab and Oberon ride, the queen on Duck Percheron and her consort on a zebra I don't recognize. Beside them stomp four scorched, tattered golems, one of them headless, one of them missing an arm, together bearing the palanquin in which rides the Legate of Heaven. He looks really irritated, and I wonder if he's particularly upset with me. Maybe he's mad that his golems got so banged up, but I don't really feel like that was my fault. Not entirely. Finally, bringing up the rear, come Rangers and Wild Things in two loose columns, bristling with spears. The Queendom is marching to war—spattered in mud, wounded, bedraggled, and completely pissed off.

Above them shines the bright star I noticed before. It looks enormous, almost like a tiny moon.

"*Mierda.*"

Behind me, I hear a scraping sound, and then I feel a warmer, drier wind on the back of my neck. I stumble out of the way, Mike Bass and I leaning on each other for balance, as the great double doors of the main entrance of Hell swing open.

A doorkeeper emerges.

He's beautiful. He's almost tall enough to fill the doorway, and he looks like a human. Like one of Homer's old Greeks, actually, with curving helmet, greaves on his legs, a breastplate, a kilt, and a spear. He has hair like mine, long and white, and just a hint of a smile on his face. Other than his size, the only thing about him that looks inhuman are the enormous birdlike talons that sprout out from the bottom of his greaves and grip the stone floor fiercely, gouging out chips at each step.

"Welcome." His voice is deep and grave. I don't know who he's talking to, but he bows, and a long cape sweeps out behind him. "You are expected."

That isn't funny. That isn't funny at all.

About the Author

D.J. Butler (Dave) is a novelist living in the Rocky Mountain northwest. His training is in law, and he worked as a securities lawyer at a major international firm and in house at two multinational semiconductor manufacturers before taking up writing fiction.

Dave writes speculative fiction for all audiences. In addition to his steampunk, urban fantasy, and science fiction novels published with WordFire Press, he has a steampunk fantasy series published by Knopf; start following The Extraordinary Journeys of Clockwork Charlie with *The Kidnap Plot*. He is also the author of the epic fantasy *Witchy Eye* (Baen, forthcoming).

Dave is a lover of language and languages, a guitarist and self-recorder, and a serious reader. He is married to a powerful and clever woman, and together they have three devious children.

Read about Dave's writing projects at davidjohnbutler.com.

IF YOU LIKED ...

If you liked *This World is Not My Home*, you might also enjoy:

Quincy J. Allen

Chemical Burn
Blood Ties

Josh Vogt

Enter the Janitor
Maids of Wrath

Other WordFire Press Titles by D.J. Butler

City of the Saints
Crecheling

Rock Band Fights Evil:

Hellhound on My Trail
Snake Handlin' Man
Crow Jane
Devil Sent the Rain

Our list of other WordFire Press authors and titles is always growing. To find out more and to see our selection of titles, visit us at:

wordfirepress.com